Twelve Palominos

A BRIG ELLIS TALE

Also by Joe Kilgore

Insomniac: Short Stories for Long Nights

Misfortune's Wake

More Brig Ellis Tales:

Fool's Errand

Cast Them Dead

Carrion Moon

Twelve Palominos

A BRIG ELLIS TALE

JOE KILGORE

Encircle Publications
Farmington, Maine, U.S.A.

TWELVE PALOMINOS Copyright © 2024 Joe Kilgore

Paperback ISBN 13: 978-1-64599-556-2
eBook ISBN 13: 978-1-64599-557-9

Library of Congress Catalog Number: 2024942934

ALL RIGHTS RESERVED. In accordance with the U.S. Copyright Act of 1976, no part of this publication may be reproduced, distributed, or transmitted in any form or by any means, or stored in a database or retrieval system, without prior written permission of the publisher, Encircle Publications, Farmington, ME.

This book is a work of fiction. All names, characters, places and events are either products of the author's imagination or are used fictitiously.

Editor: Cynthia Brackett-Vincent

Book design: Deirdre Wait

Cover design: Christopher Wait
Cover photograph © Getty Images

Published by:

Encircle Publications
PO Box 187
Farmington, ME 04938

http://encirclepub.com
info@encirclepub.com

For
Claudia, Jezebel, Woolrich, & Moonpie

"There are only two tragedies in life: one is not getting what one wants, and the other is getting it."

—Oscar Wilde

PROLOGUE

1984 / Dharan, Saudi Arabia

A Korean guest worker tells an American drilling engineer that The Stander is in a display case at a gold store in the city. For the right price, the Korean agrees to steal it. The deal is made. The heist successful. The American leaves on the next flight. The Korean however, is later recognized by the store owner, arrested, and made to confess. The following day, at a public ceremony, his hands are lopped off.

1986 / Beijing, China

Fen Lee, a low level bureaucrat in the Ministry of Tourism agrees to part with The Walker. Kept surreptitiously in his family for decades, he accepts the American's price but demands absolute silence on how he attained it. Days later, the American is gone and Fen Lee is unceremoniously imprisoned. There are no secrets in Communist China.

1990 / Cairo, Egypt
A street vendor at the Khan El Khalili market stealthily hands over The Prancer to the American's representative. The brokered sale calls for the disposal of the go-between. Among the noise and clamor of the market, the removal of the vendor is accomplished quickly and quietly, but not without considerable loss of blood.

1993 / Mumbai, India
At the train station, the tall Sikh reaches into his dastaar where he has hidden The Loper. He passes it to the American's agent who will make sure it reaches the United States. Afterwards, the train carrying the Sikh back to his village derails, tumbling down a hillside. All in his car are killed.

1997 / London, England
On a bench in Hyde Park, two men discuss Tony Blair and the Labor Party's landslide victory as one man hands the other a small box containing The Galloper. When they depart, the American takes the Concorde back to New York and the Englishman returns to his office in Whitehall. There he experiences a severe myocardial infarction and drops dead at his desk.

2001 / Istanbul, Turkey

At an upscale Hammam, the American enjoys a body scrub, wash, and massage. Afterwards, he dresses and finds The Kicker wrapped in a silk scarf in the inside breast pocket of his suit. Leaving, he thanks the owner and hands him a gift-wrapped package concealing a copious amount of cash. A month later fire consumes the bathhouse and burns it and its proprietor to ashes.

2006 / Bangkok, Thailand

A bar girl plies her trade and lets the American's man buy her multiple rum and Cokes. Then she takes him to a short-time hotel where they have sex and swap The Grazer for a handbag stuffed with thousand dollar bills. The next morning, he's gone. She returns the money to her boss, who returns it to his boss, who directs that the bar girl be instructed to keep the transaction a secret… permanently.

2008 / Rio de Janeiro, Brazil

Strolling Ipanema beach, the American nods to the bikini-clad women he passes. One slips a note in his hand instructing him to meet a Portuguese man with a patch over his eye below Christ the Redeemer statue at four in the afternoon. At the meet, the American passes a camera case loaded with cash to the one-eyed Portuguese who hands him a small leather pouch with The Pawer inside. Six months later, in an automobile accident, the Brazilian loses his other eye.

2013 / Marseille, France

A sailor leaves his freighter and taxis to the La Quai Du Rire. He picks up a pre-purchased ticket and takes his seat on the aisle as the comedy begins. The American's emissary sits next to him and they exchange The Kneeler for the agreed upon price. The sailor makes it back to the ship, but two days into his next voyage he is stabbed in a boiler room knife fight and soon expires from sepsis.

2015 / Bogotá, Colombia

In a heavily guarded hacienda, the cartel captain surrounds The Leaper in cocaine and encloses it in a shipment bound for the United States. A Cessna pilot flies it to a deserted runway outside Brownsville, Texas, where it's checked by the American's hired authenticator. It will then be driven across country to its final destination. On his way back to Colombia, the pilot encounters a thunderstorm, loses his bearings, and fatally crashes into a mountainside.

2020 / Berlin, Germany

The American and a striking blonde fräulein traverse the mile-long section of the Berlin Wall known as the East Side Gallery. They talk discreetly as they take in the graffiti, murals, and artwork that memorialize the spirit that infected the city during unification. When they part, he has The Lander—eleventh of The Twelve Palominos. She has the money, but also the initial stages of the Covid virus which will lead to her untimely death only weeks later.

2024 / San Diego, California

A man, appropriately named Broadhurst, smuggles The Riser into the States.

CHAPTER 1

LIKE A LOT OF TOWNS with manicured sites for tourists but dirt under their civic fingernails, San Diego had its share of dive bars. Not the remakes with websites, ladies' night, and happy hour. Rather, the ones with scarred mahogany, split Naugahyde, and hours that couldn't accurately be described as happy since the Reagan administration. The Four Aces was one of the latter. The watering hole was an anachronistic eye-sore wedged between warehouses and bait shops on Harbor Drive. It had somehow withstood the onslaught of gentrification that seemed to be spreading like a flesh eating disease—the flesh of the working classes who didn't know what anachronism or gentrification meant, but they sure as hell knew change when they saw it. That's why The Four Aces was able to maintain its profitability. Those on the losing end of life's ever-changing lottery tend to routinely wash their defeat down with strong drink or cheap beer. Both were served liberally to luckless patrons more than satisfied to soak their troubles in a soothing balm of non-judgmental booze.

On this particular day, however, there was one there who differed from the regular clientele. He had on a suit with no tie and wore his thirty-nine years like a man much younger. Close-cropped hair, chiseled chin and a face that looked lived-in rather than ravaged, tended to set him apart. Aware that he was likely to stand out among the misfits and miscreants that normally frequented The Four Aces, he had taken the last stool on the short corner of the long bar. It was out of the sight line of most customers, off the bartender's regular loop, and about as private as anywhere in the place except the toilet. That's why Brig Ellis chose it, and that's why he was still nursing a Modelo that he had ordered a half hour ago. Unlike the others there, he hadn't come to drink. He had come to watch another man drink and to see who the fellow might be drinking with. So far it was no one. Just as it had been for the last couple of days.

Ellis didn't like divorce work. Normally, he didn't take that kind of job. But Edith's sob story sucked him in. Had two kids at home, she said. Couldn't make ends meet as it was. Feared Bob was seeing some bimbo on the side and wasting what little money they had on suds and sex in the afternoon. Not necessarily in that order. Would he look into it for her? She could pay him in installments. So much a week. For as many weeks as it took. She had to know who it was. So she could take him to court and hopefully get alimony for her and the kids. Even though Ellis's card read

INVESTIGATIONS, SECURITY, CONFIDENTIAL MATTERS, he seldom stooped to snooping on philandering husbands or wives. But there was something about Edith's plight that brought out the soft touch in the hard-nosed private investigator. *Damn*, he thought, is she going to be surprised.

For three days Ellis had been at the docks when Bob finished his shift. He followed him from the time he left work until he returned home. Not once had the supposedly wayward husband stopped to put his hands on anything resembling what old timers used to call a floozy. The only thing Bob lovingly gripped were the tequila shots served one after the other until he returned to his car and surprisingly made it safely to his driveway. Bob may have been guzzling every bit of their discretionary income and more, but he wasn't cheating on Edith. She was scheduled to come to Ellis's office the following morning. He planned to surprise her with the news.

The next day, when Edith arrived on time at Ellis's less-than-pretentious but more-than-poverty-row office, she wasn't alone. There was a man with her that she introduced as Mr. Skeffington. Late thirties or early forties, Ellis guessed. The P.I. took note of the Brooks Brothers three-piece gray suit. It enhanced what appeared to be a barrel chest and a body maintained as well as his attire. He even carried a black Homburg which he had removed just before entering. His adherence to manners allowed Ellis to observe more closely the man's coif and facial features. His hair was platinum, except for the roots. But it was razor cut and stylish and gave the impression it likely once topped a uniform. He had a strait nose, high cheekbones, thin lips and cobalt blue eyes beneath brows that matched his neatly combed hair. It was a serious, no nonsense face, with a definite hint of menace behind the eyes. The man perused Ellis as fully as he himself was being observed, but said nothing as he and Edith took seats in the two chairs fronting the P. I.'s desk.

"You may speak candidly, Mr. Ellis," Edith said somberly. "What did you find?"

Looking first to Skeffington, then quickly back to Edith, Ellis said, "Your husband spends his time drinking more than he… or probably anyone for that matter… should, but he does it alone. There is no *other woman*."

"Now, Mr. Ellis, I want you to be sure of things, you know. I mean, well, perhaps you should keep surveilling him for a while. Just to be positive. Simply keep track of your time and I'll find a way to pay you… for as long as it takes, really."

"There's no point, Edith. He's not cheating on you. He is drinking heavily. Something's definitely bothering him. But he seems to be looking for answers in the bottom of a glass, not in the arms of another woman. You should try to get him to open up. It looks like he needs to talk to someone.

Can't think of any reason it shouldn't be you."

"Oh, well, that is something isn't it?" She began. "All right, then. I'll just pay you for what you've done up to now. How much will that be?"

"No charge," Ellis replied.

"What? That's not fair… to you. I mean you spent time watching him and—"

"I wasn't working any other cases," Ellis interjected, "so it didn't take time away from something else. And there are really no expenses of any consequence. Your husband's spending money on alcohol that could probably be better spent elsewhere. Why don't you talk to him about it. Maybe you can help with whatever's causing his behavior. Use what you would have paid me on something for your kids. Try to get your family back on track."

"This is so generous of you, Mr. Ellis. I mean I can't—"

Cutting her off in mid-sentence, Skeffington said to the woman, "That's enough. You may go now."

Edith's mouth closed immediately. There wasn't the slightest effort to object. She simply smiled politely, gathered her purse under her arm, rose, and without uttering another word, left the office.

Ellis looked at Skeffington. "What am I missing here?"

"The woman who just left is not named Edith. Bob is not the name of the man you've been following. They are not married. They're both actors. Hired to play the respective roles you've witnessed over the last few days."

Ellis picked up a slight accent in Skeffington's voice. A trace of Irish perhaps. But that assumption couldn't compete for space in his brain with his primary vexation. "So just what the hell is going on?"

"You were being tested, Mr. Ellis."

"Oh, really. Did I pass?"

"I believe the phrase is… with flying colors."

Ellis held his tongue, waiting for more information. Skeffington waited longer. The pause was in danger of elongating even more.

"Are you going to tell me what this is all about? Or are you just going to sit there until I get mad enough to toss you out on your ass?"

"Your curiosity would probably keep you from doing that. And if it didn't, I would. But you are owed an explanation."

"Agreed. In fact, I may be owed more than that. But let's start with the explanation and we'll go from there."

Skeffington crossed his legs, rested his Homburg on his knee and began. "The little charade you've been part of was initiated to see exactly what sort of man you are."

"Is that a fact? And what sort of man am I?"

"Apparently an honest man. One might even say honorable."

"Because I didn't charge her?"

"Because you not only didn't charge her for work you actually performed, but also because you didn't take advantage of her by accepting more work—and therefore more fees—that you knew to be unnecessary."

"So I'm a straight shooter and a nice guy. You could have found that out by asking around."

"We did. We spoke with acquaintances of yours in the police department. And of course we looked into your background."

"Really," Ellis said. "How'd you do that?"

"We have extensive contacts."

"You do? Well pray tell, what did you learn?"

"We learned that you joined the military right out of high school. Received outstanding marks in fitness tests and weapons use. Volunteered for paratrooper and Ranger training. Saw combat in a number of Middle East hot spots. Engaged in classified operations as well. Clandestine assignments that called for both secrecy and lethality. You mustered out after putting in your twenty years, leaving you a relatively young retiree who routinely turns down extensive offers from private security firms because you prefer to work for yourself. Work that… in addition to your army pension… provides an income some would consider reasonable, but most would consider modest. Yet you prefer the freedom to be your own man, so to speak."

"Learned all that, did you. And it still wasn't enough?"

"Thoroughness told us what you *were*, Mr. Ellis. We needed to find out what you are now."

"Just who is this *us* and *we* you've been referring to. Is there a rabbit under your hat?"

"No. There is only myself and my employer."

"Who is?"

"Someone who wants you to accept an assignment."

"Which is?"

"Like your business card advertises… a confidential matter."

Ellis paused for a moment before responding. He had found Skeffington's subterfuge interesting initially, but had since tired of it. "One… I don't do things that are illegal. Two… if I accept a job, I determine the compensation. Three… I never agree to anything before I know what it entails. So, now that you've spent all this time on research, interrogation, and amateur theatrics… just what is it precisely that you want me to do… and who would I be doing it for?"

"My employer prefers to speak with you personally about that."

"Good. Have him come in tomorrow."

"He doesn't come to you. You go to him." Then Skeffington reached in his vest pocket, pulled out a small white card and put it on the desk in front of Ellis. The card had an address on it, but no name. Turning, and walking toward the door, he said, "Noon tomorrow. Be on time. He appreciates punctuality."

"Who doesn't?" Ellis quipped.

With his hand on the doorknob, Skeffington said, "Rest assured, Mr. Ellis, your financial compensation will be extremely rewarding."

What a pretentious prick, Ellis thought, and quickly said, "Look. No name, no show. Who's your employer?"

"C. Tyler McCullum."

Silence lay in the air for all of a millisecond.

"You don't say. I'll be there."

CHAPTER 2

THERE WAS NOT A LOT of countryside that was still countryside northeast of San Diego. But most of what there was belonged to C. Tyler McCullum. As Ellis drove his classic Mercedes 230 SL coupe through the heart of it, he continued to wonder why one of the country's wealthiest individuals would want to see him. He had started wondering about it the minute Skeffington left his office the day before. He had ruminated over it the rest of the afternoon and during the dinner he had alone at Benny's on the beach. He even lost a good half-hour of sleep mulling it over as he lay in bed before finally nodding off. He'd yet to come up with anything resembling a reasonable answer.

Ellis knew what most people knew about McCullum. His name was seldom absent from the pages of business websites, the rankings of America's richest tycoons, or the published guest lists of high society and charity soirees. It had become common knowledge that he made his fortune in oil, and even though he was one of the last of the old school wildcatters, he had made the transition to natural gas and even wind farming without retarding in the least the growth of his embarrassingly obscene financial holdings. Ellis had the impression that McCullum didn't seek the public eye, but neither did he hide from it. The P. I. bet the septuagenarian enjoyed seeing his name still being bandied about with the likes of the somewhat younger Gates, Bezos, and Musk.

Ellis had used his phone's destination app to provide directions for the address on the card that Skeffington had given him. He had no intention of ever installing any sort of after-market device that would do the same thing in his car. Spoiling a classic for the sake of convenience simply wasn't in his DNA. He figured if he could walk and chew gum at the same time, he could also keep his eyes on the road while he kept his ears on the recorded voice giving him directions. Having left the main highway some time ago for a paved road that meandered through softly rolling hills, Ellis came upon a gate, apparently still some distance from his destination as no house was yet visible. The gate had both a squawk box and a camera mounted on it. As he looked up at the equipment, Ellis wondered if he was under observation. He was.

"Mr. Brig Ellis?" The squawk box asked.

"What if I said no."

"Levity is inappropriate."

Wow, Ellis thought. *Put in my place by an unseen but apparently omnipotent being. Better play it straight.* "Yes. Brig Ellis to see Mr. McCullum."

"You're late."

Ellis looked at his watch. It read 11:55. "It's not noon yet," he said.

"You're not here yet," the box replied.

"How long does it take to get from where I am to where you are," Ellis asked.

"Ten minutes."

"I'll make it in five."

The gate swung open and Ellis put petal to metal. He traversed the winding road that led up the hill like Mario Andretti overdosing on exhaust fumes and caffeine. Why he was risking life and limb to keep from being five minutes late was beyond him, but he was committed. Twisting, turning, tires squealing around curves, and his engine roaring in the straightaways, Ellis managed to barrel onto the circular drive fronting the gigantic three-story house with thirty seconds to spare. He hustled out of his car, slammed the door behind him and rushed toward the front of the mansion. As he reached for the decorative gold doorknocker in the shape of a horse's rear end, and before he could use the tail to announce his presence, the door opened from the inside.

"Good day, Mr. Ellis," Skeffington said. "Nice of you to be on time."

"No problem," the P. I. replied, hiding as best he could his heaving chest.

"Right this way," Skeffington gestured. As he led Ellis under the soaring entryway and down the long corridor that bisected a massive dining room on one side and a combination study and library on the other, the P. I. noticed that today the fellow was wearing a dark jacket over gray pants which could be viewed as the uniform of a new age butler. *Odd*, Ellis thought to himself. He had assumed the man held a somewhat higher position. Reaching the leaded glass doors at the rear of the house, Skeffington opened one and motioned toward a table for two that had been set up on a marble patio fronting a glistening thirty-yard by thirty-foot rectangular swimming pool of azure blue water.

"Mr. McCullum is on the phone. He will join you directly. There is water and a chilled Pouilly-Fuissé on the table."

"Thanks," Ellis responded. Then, unable to help himself, he added, "Will Mr. McCullum be long? I appreciate punctuality."

Skeffington locked eyes with the P. I. and stared silently for a moment bereft of smile or frown, then simply turned and walked away.

Ellis moved toward the table but didn't sit down, wondering if the lord of the manor had a particular seat that he preferred. The P. I. wasn't totally without consideration, manners, and one or two social graces. He didn't mind standing for a while and simply taking in the view. Beyond the long, shimmering pool, stood a huge black and white stable, and beyond that, acres and acres of pasture land latticed by white fencing both sturdy and decorative. Ellis hadn't been waiting long when he heard the murmur of voices some distance behind him. He turned and saw Skeffington and another man conversing at the home's rear entrance. Their conversation ended as Skeffington went back into the house and C. Tyler McCullum headed his way.

McCullum was a big man, well over six feet. He was gangly and his gait reminiscent of an orangutan Ellis had once seen in an old Clint Eastwood movie. A weathered Stetson Silver Belly hat sat atop his head doing its best to cover white tufts of unruly hair that protruded over each ear. His cream shirt was striped on each side by suspenders that held his tan trousers in place around a belly that signaled satisfaction more than gluttony. The closer he came to Ellis, the easier it was for the P.I. to make out the man's face. It was long, like a horse's. Deep set vertical lines etched his ruddy cheeks and sizable bags sat below dark topaz eyes. His mouth was wide and as he removed an enormous cigar from it, a slight gap was revealed between large front teeth.

"Hello, Mr. Ellis, I'm Tyler McCullum." The voice was almost other worldly. Low not loud, but sonorous, imposing, almost grandiloquent without seeming to try.

Involuntarily, Ellis cleared his own voice before he spoke and extended his hand. "Good day, sir."

As they shook hands, each took note of the other's grip. McCullum recorded the heft and pressure of the P.I.'s; Ellis, the cracked, dry, elephant like skin of the elder man.

"Glad you could join me today," McCullum said, motioning to the table beside the pool.

"Had an opening in my schedule," Ellis said, smiling, as he and his host each took a seat.

"Busy man, are you, Mr. Ellis?"

"Well, you should know, sir. Since you've had an eye on me for the last couple of days."

"Yes. Sorry about that. But a man in my position needs to know all he can about someone he wants to do business with. Care for a glass of wine," he asked, raising the bottle.

"I would."

McCullum half-filled Ellis's glass and his own, then said, "Here's to mutual benefit. Cheers."

"Cheers," Ellis responded, and each took a drink.

"Very good," Ellis said. "Of course, I assumed it would be."

"Wine, Mr. Ellis, is proof that God loves us and wants us to be happy."

"Ben Franklin, right? Though I actually heard that quote attributed to beer."

"Plagiarized no doubt, to raise one's stature among those he or she was drinking with. Mine was an abbreviation of the actual quote, which is, *'Behold the rain which descends from heaven upon our vineyards, and which incorporates with the grapes to be changed into wine; a constant proof that God loves us, and loves to see us happy'.*"

Ellis nodded, raised his glass toward McCullum, and spoke before taking another drink. "I stand corrected."

"As will we all," the elder man said, "when we stand before our Maker."

As Ellis was pondering whether or not McCullum actually believed his last statement, Skeffington came from the house. This time he was robed in a satin dressing gown and carrying a large silver platter. Arriving at their table, he removed the cover and set it on a trolley nearby. Then with his bare hands, he took a plate for each man, held them momentarily while the two moved their linens from the table to their laps, then slowly placed them in front of each man. Ellis thought the swordfish steaks with asparagus and wild rice looked delicious.

"Thank you, Mr. Skeffington," McCullum said. "Feel free to proceed with your exercise regimen. I'm sure Mr. Ellis won't mind."

Before McCullum's guest could agree or disagree, Skeffington walked to the pool, removed his robe, and placed it on a nearby lounge. Then he stood at the edge of the pool clad only in a white Speedo. Putting his feet together, he executed a virtual perpendicular dive that sent him swimming away. But not before Ellis had looked on with some degree of envy at the tanned and sculpted body, seemingly shaped from marble without a trace of fat, but with scars the P. I. recognized—scars that appeared to be the result of blade and bullet wounds. Ellis then inched his chair a bit closer to the table and absentmindedly reached out to move his plate nearer.

"Whoa!" Ellis yelped, as his fingertips jerked back to his sides like a gunslinger in reverse.

"Oh, sorry," McCullum said, "should have mentioned that plate is hot. I'll take no offence if you want to soothe those digits with a bit of cold water."

"Think I will," Ellis said, as he dipped his linen in his water glass, then wrapped the cloth momentarily around his throbbing fingers. "Didn't seem to trouble him, though. Picked them both up without a word… even held them a second before putting them on the table."

"Yes. Well, you see that wouldn't bother Mr. Skeffington. He suffers from CIPA… congenital insensitivity to pain. It's a disease caused by a genetic mutation preventing the formation of nerve cells which send signals of pain, heat and cold to the brain. A rare disorder. Approximately one in 25,000 or less are affected by it. He has to be quite careful, you know. Just because he feels no pain doesn't mean he's not susceptible to infection, blood loss, that sort of thing. His vital organs are as vulnerable as yours or mine. The difference being, you could cut one of his kidneys out sans anesthetic and he wouldn't feel a thing. But without proper post-surgical care he could expire just like any other man."

"I'm a little confused. I mean, what is his actual role? When he was in my office, I thought perhaps he was your attorney. Then when I arrived today, he seemed to be your butler. Now that he's making laps in the pool, I have to ask myself what he really does for you?"

"Mr. Skeffington performs a number of functions. Not the least of which is security. He actually suggested that he'd be amenable to performing multiple tasks. I readily agreed as it enables me to have fewer people under foot. I trust him implicitly. He's been with me for years. It's almost like he's a member of the family. That's why I give him the run of the place and indulge his occasionally eccentric exercise routines. He'll do a hundred laps before stopping to clear away our lunch… which we should partake of before it's gets cold."

"I'm not sure there's any danger of that."

CHAPTER 3

OVER LUNCH, McCULLUM REGALED HIS guest with stories of his rags to riches rise from oil field roustabout to roughneck to derrickman to driller. Ellis got the impression the old man was prouder of the manual labor he muscled through as a youth than the economic exploits he oversaw which took him from wildcatter to oil baron. Then seemingly out of nowhere, his host said, "People sometimes ask me what the C in C. Tyler McCullum stands for."

"Do you ever tell them?"

"Almost never. But I'll tell you, Mr. Ellis. It stands for Clarence."

"Well... I can see why you might prefer Tyler. Seems to suit you better."

"I've always thought so. I tell people I was named after John Tyler, America's tenth president. The first man to ascend to the presidency without being elected to the office. Served almost a full term after the untimely death of William Henry Harrison. Tyler presided over the United States annexation of Texas, you know."

"I have to admit that I did not know that."

"Well, now you're smarter than you were when you came here."

"Guess I am," Ellis replied. "But I'm not smart enough."

"Smart enough for what?"

"Smart enough to know why. Why you laid out this tasty spread… why you shared your little intimacy regarding your name… why you're going out of your way to charm me when you could have just come to my office, dropped a wad of dough on my desk, and told me what you wanted."

"Had I done that, would you have acquiesced?"

"Certainly not… at least, until I heard the specifics."

"That's the point. If I had just tried to run roughshod over you, your manliness and your pride would have demanded that you give me the boot. But now, you've drunk my wine, eaten my food, learned of my hideous first name… now you think you owe me. Thus I have a bit of leverage over you."

"A bit perhaps. But I'm still interested in the specifics."

"That's one of the problems with your generation, Mr. Ellis. Too impatient. Can't wait to get on with things. Even when you don't know what they are. Tell you what. Indulge me just a bit more and we'll get to the heart of the matter. Fear not, by the way. You won't walk away empty-handed, whatever you decide. I'm going to pay you for the time you spent on our bogus divorce drama.

You certainly deserve it."

"I told Edith… rather, I told the actress you hired that there was no charge and there isn't. I'm not going to go back on that simply because you have deeper pockets."

"That's why I wanted you, Mr. Ellis. A man who sticks by his guns. Not very many around these days. Come. Take a walk with me."

Leaving the table, McCullum offered one of the extra cigars he had in his shirt pocket to Ellis. The P.I. declined. The elder lit one for himself, then began strolling to the stable with Ellis in tow.

As they neared the stable, McCullum said, "Ah, the smell of fresh manure. Nothing quite like it. Unmistakable in its honesty and utter disregard for anything other than relief."

"Never quite thought about it that way," Ellis responded. "But it's definitely fragrant."

"Things that come from inside us are the true things, you know. Tears, and blood, and the stench of waste… we can't hide those… like we hide just about everything else in life."

At the end of the stable, wide doors opened into a corral. McCullum stopped before moving toward the only animal occupying it. Ellis stood beside him.

"Like to introduce you to someone, Mr. Ellis. This magnificent animal is Emperado."

The gorgeous horse stood sixteen hands high, his golden color outshone only by a snow white mane and tail. He looked directly at the two men looking at him, as if to see who would blink first.

Ellis said, "Magnificent is the right word, alright. Always been fascinated by palominos."

"As has most of the world throughout history," McCullum began. "They're said to have originated in Spain, or perhaps the Middle East. Desert land, nevertheless. So they'd blend in with the sand's color… protecting themselves from predators and the harsh rays of the sun. Nobility has always been attracted to palominos. Queen Isabella of Spain kept several to ride, and when she sent her exploration to the new world she included a stallion and five mares. Those horses provided the initial stock for palominos in North America."

"The golden color is definitely regal," Ellis commented.

"Indeed," McCullum agreed. Adding swiftly, "Often attained by breeding a chestnut with a buckskin. Emperado is the stallion who will sire my herd. He's even more spirited than he looks. The only human he lets ride him is my daughter. Kindred spirits, they appear to be. Right now, Emperado is taking his daily constitutional. Let's leave him to it. Anyway, I have ten more I'd like to show you."

"Ten? Really? Where do you keep them?"

"In the house, of course. Let's go have a look."

Ellis assumed the old man was pulling his leg. But as McCullum quickened his pace toward the gigantic home, the P. I. willingly parked his disbelief and swiftly followed.

Inside, the elder led the way to his study, a room that could easily be mistaken for a branch of the public library. Floor to ceiling shelves housed row upon row of books neatly standing shoulder to shoulder with no space available for anything resembling objets d'art. However, on one side of a massive oaken desk, a six-foot celestial mahogany floor globe stood vigil, and on the other side, a prodigious redwood stand in the shape of a crown was topped with a long horizontal glass case. Inside that case, there appeared to be miniature horses. Ten of them. All palominos. All with sparkling green eyes.

"Come, have a look, Mr. Ellis. And if you're not sure, let me tell you what you're seeing."

"Well, I'm seeing horses. Pretty small though, almost like toys."

"Very insightful. They are indeed toys. But not just any toys. These were the toys of a god."

McCullum let his comment hang in the air. When he didn't follow up, Ellis did.

"All right. You've got my interest. Tell me about the toys, and the god."

Pointing to a red leather chair in front of his desk,

McCullum said, "Have a seat, Mr. Ellis. This might take a moment."

The P. I. sat and McCullum began.

"Are you familiar with China's Qing dynasty?"

"No. Can't really say that I am."

"The Qing dynasty ruled China for almost four hundred years. Probably would have actually made four hundred, maybe more, had it not been for the Xinhai Revolution, the Sino-Japanese conflict and a couple of World Wars. But I digress. Point being, the last Qing dynasty emperor was named Puyi. Though mortal, as you and I would see it, the Chinese looked upon him as immortal… a gift from heaven… a god on earth. And even though he became emperor at the age of two, he was still seen as the supreme leader in all things. Nothing was too good, too outlandish, too expensive for this child god. That included his toys."

"At a parade one day, the little emperor saw a beautiful palomino stallion that had previously been sent to his grandmother, the Dowager Queen. So enamored was he with the horse that it was decided he should have toy horses to play with. Immediately, artisans were called upon to create the world's most beautiful horse. Most designs were rejected because they were too big for the emperor's tiny hands. Then they hit upon it. Not just one horse. But many. Not just toys to be tossed and forgotten, but toys to be unequaled and passed from one emperor to the next. These... the very horses you see here... are those Palominos."

McCullum stood beside the glass case and used his cigar to point as he continued to talk.

"They were carved from the rarest alabaster—the stone hailed by ancient Egyptians as The Stone of the Sun Gods. The golden color was achieved by paint derived from vegetable and mineral oils. Each horse was imbued with vibrantly spectacular eyes of precious emeralds. And, as you can see, each was created in its own unique pose—standing, walking, prancing, loping, galloping, kicking, grazing, pawing, kneeling, leaping, landing, and rising up in the wind with its mane and tail flowing."

McCullum paused to take a deep drag from his cigar. As he blew out the smoke, Ellis jumped in.

"You just mentioned twelve positions. But there are only ten horses."

"Please, you're getting ahead of yourself... and me."

"Sorry."

"The dozen palominos immediately became the rarest toys in the world," McCullum continued. "But the young emperor's time with them was not to last. Political unrest increased, violence began to spot the landscape. Even within the walls of the Forbidden City, chaos was cresting. The emperor's servants, all eunuchs, began to vanish.

Precious objects were stolen and sold on the black market to fund escapes. One by one, the palominos were lost to the tumultuous times. The dynasty ended, as T. S. Eliot so eloquently put it, *not with a bang, but with a whimper*, and the fabled palominos went their separate ways.

"Mr. Ellis, for the last forty of my seventy-eight years on this planet, I have attempted to recover the twelve palominos. Forty years of scouring records, running down rumors, expending enormous sums of money, and in some cases, even stealing if necessary, to unite them under my roof. For whatever reason, men are consumed by obsessions… mine has been to acquire the toys created for a god. That obsession only grew stronger in the last few years with the birth of my grandson, Tanner. He's four years old now. Two years older than the emperor, Puyi, when the palominos were created. I am more determined than ever to have them, and to leave them to my grandson when I depart this earthly realm."

"And… per my earlier comment… I assume you only have the ten."

"So, by your powers of observation, it might seem. The fact is, the eleventh is virtually within my grasp."

Again, that damned pregnant pause arose and the P. I. knew he was expected to ask.

"And the twelfth?"

"That's where you come in, Mr. Ellis."

CHAPTER 4

MCCULLUM STOOD AND GAZED OUT the study's massive picture window. Ellis sat and waited for his host to continue. As he turned to face his guest, the sun's rays poured through the glass and rimmed McCullum in backlight, creating an actual glow around the man. Ellis had a gut feeling that this wasn't a mere coincidence of time and space, but rather an affect that the old man had probably stumbled on before and used occasionally to make himself and his words more impactful. He had to admit though, it was dramatic.

"Mr. Ellis, I want you to help me recover the twelfth palomino."

Ellis responded with a question. "And just what might that involve?"

"Not much, really. You would simply serve as my emissary... a go-between, if you like... to attain the palomino and bring it to me."

"Why do you need a go-between? Why isn't this something you can do yourself?"

"In this case, unfortunately, my reputation precedes me. If the individual who has the palomino were to know he was doing business with me, the price would likely quadruple."

"And what exactly is the price?"

"Five million dollars."

Ellis paused momentarily before responding. Then asked, "If the thing is that valuable… why doesn't the current owner simply take it to one of the big auction houses? Maybe get even more for it."

"A public auction would require records. Official records of ownership, bill of sales, that sort of thing."

"So, whoever has it now… didn't necessarily pay for it?"

"Oh, I'm sure payment in some form was extracted, Mr. Ellis. But it wasn't necessarily coin of the realm. If you get my meaning."

"Where is this individual, and the palomino now?"

"That's the good news. He and it are right here in San Diego. Though only just recently arrived."

The next ten minutes were spent with McCullum explaining in detail what would be expected of Ellis. The explanation sounded way too simple. As he listened to the instructions he was being given, he was simultaneously thinking about what he wasn't being told. Cash however, has a way of throwing caution to the wind.

"And for your participation," McCullum summed up, "I suggest a fee of fifty thousand dollars. You can leave here today with a check for half. The other half to be paid when you bring the palomino to me."

Ellis was gob smacked, but he held his astonishment in check, if not his honesty. "That's only about ten times the fee I was thinking about."

"I'm sure it sounds like a king's ransom to you, Mr. Ellis, but it's a mere pittance to me. And if you bring this off without complications, you will have earned it."

"Your instructions didn't sound all that complicated."

"Yes. Well you see, it's not just what you have to do. It's who you have to deal with. The people involved are… let's say… less than scrupulous. One might even call some of them… potentially dangerous. And then there's the secretive nature of the assignment. You can't let them know that I'm your client. You can't let any authorities know the nature of the item you're trying to acquire. Even if something goes awry. And there is one more thing."

"Story of my life," Ellis quipped. "Seems like there's always one more thing."

"Be that as it may, I didn't want you to find out later and be concerned that I didn't mention it."

"Didn't mention what?"

"The curse. The Curse of the Twelve Palominos. An old wives' tale, I suspect. But it's been around since the eunuchs started absconding with the miniatures. It is said that Puyi put a curse on the ponies and that whomever acquires one by nefarious means will be met with a hideous death... and should someone of ignoble nature acquire the lot... disaster will be visited upon all mankind."

"You apparently don't buy into that?"

"The people from whence the curse sprang believed that Puyi was a god, and a curse from a god must surely be true. But, Puyi wasn't a god, Mr. Ellis. He was merely a man like you or me. The curse is simply a myth, employed to intimidate those who would seek to acquire the palominos. So tell me now, can I count on you?"

The two men concluded their business. Skeffington, now dressed again as Ellis had seen him upon arrival, showed the P. I. to the door. When Ellis walked out to get into his two-seater that would take him back to the city, he couldn't help but notice that one seat was occupied.

"I understand you're going into San Diego. Can you give me a lift?"

"I've got a feeling you know this already, but my name is Brig Ellis."

"And my name is Alexis McCullum."

"I could have guessed."

The resemblance to her father was oddly remarkable. Her long nose was straighter and came to a finer point. Her mouth was big but her lips were full and sensual. Ellis didn't know what color the old man's hair once was, but hers was flaming auburn and fell past her shoulders.

When she spoke he noticed that she didn't have the gap between her teeth. Probably fixed long ago, he assumed. And her eyes… he actually couldn't remember what color McCullum's eyes were, but hers were emerald green and shone like the precious stone eyes of the palominos. On occasion, life can be remarkably kind, he thought to himself. Somehow she was the spitting image of her old man, but where he was at best ill-favored, she was a knockout. He even found her freckles beguiling.

"My car's in the shop. If you could drop me off, I'd appreciate it."

"Happy to help," Ellis responded. Then he started the engine, dropped the car in gear, and pulled away as she reached in her purse and put on a pair of sun glasses. His aviator shades were already on. As he wound down the path he had taken on the way in, her fiery locks blew and swirled in multiple directions, briefly putting him in mind of Medusa's snakes.

"Sorry I don't have a hat or scarf or anything like that. Want me to put the top up?"

"Certainly not," she said. "If it doesn't bother you, it doesn't bother me. Got a comb in my purse, anyway."

"Good. Cause I don't carry one of those either."

His close cropped hair revealed the reason for his comment without her having to ask. So she put a different query to him. "Like to travel light, do you?"

"As often as possible."

Silence set in for a bit. Ellis couldn't help himself from cutting his eyes her way now and then. With dark glasses covering them, he figured it wouldn't be too obvious. He figured incorrectly.

"Do I make you nervous," she asked without looking at him.

"Nervous? No. I was just wondering."

"Wondering what?"

They were just a couple of hundred yards from getting back on the main highway. Ellis slowed, pulled the car onto the shoulder of the graded road, stopped, and let the engine idle.

"Wondering when you were going to tell me why you're really here."

"Didn't buy the car repair scenario, huh."

"Nope. Yours is a lifestyle that has broken things picked up, fixed, then returned. Without minding what added costs might be involved. Interesting gambit, but not persuasive."

She turned in her seat and looked directly at Ellis. "What did my father ask you to do?"

"Can't really discuss that." He then reached in his pocket, pulled out a business card and handed it to her. "It would fall under the heading of that phrase, Confidential Matters."

She perused it and said, "Yeah, I heard father and Skeffington talking about a private investigator."

"Then why'd you ask."

"Only heard them talking about *what*, not *why*."

"Well, since I'm not going to discuss what your father and I talked about, and since there's no car that really needs to be picked up from any repair shop… want me to turn around and take you back?

"No. I'd rather you take me into town and buy me a drink."

"I see. And after, I guess I'll have to turn around and drive you back out here."

"I'll call an Uber. Or grab a taxi. I've got cab fare."

I'm sure you do, Ellis thought to himself, but didn't say. "So… care for bars on the beach?"

"Who doesn't?"

"Okay, then. First round's on me."

CHAPTER 5

BENNY'S WAS A SEASIDE JOINT just off Harbor Drive that Ellis frequented. It attracted both tourists and locals alike. Tourists found the beached boat design quaint. Locals found the drinks strong and the food tasty. Two out of three reasons Ellis was a regular. He had also done a couple of favors once for the bartender, Griff, which the drink jockey repaid by comping the P. I.'s drinks now and then. Provided he didn't have too many and provided he was alone.

Griff was a long, lean, Black man with empathy for every drinker's story and opinions he found impossible to keep to himself. Advice poured out of his mouth like a nickel slot machine paying off. Actual knowledge or personal experience with whatever subject a customer brought up was not a prerequisite for a Griff-load of advice. One only had to ask a question or share a confidence with the affable barman and he would wax eloquently on exactly what to do and how to do it. While Ellis liked the man, he was less than enamored with his verbosity. Which is why the P. I. generally maintained a strong, silent type demeanor when he was in the place.

Ellis knew he and his new client's daughter hadn't come for the ocean view. So he pointed toward a booth in the back and asked what she wanted to drink. Answer in hand, as they passed the bar he waved to Griff and said, "One scotch, one bourbon. Both neat." Griff knew Ellis didn't drink scotch and that his bourbon of choice was Woodford Reserve. So he pulled the Glenfiddich bottle down because one look at the lady told him she was used to quality. Probably a lot more used to it than Ellis. Securing the drinks, Griff walked to the booth and set them on the table. Before exiting he gave Ellis a *you're-coming-up-in-the-world* glance. The P. I. did his best to ignore it.

"Cheers."

"Cheers."

After both took a drink, she said, "I'm not very good at small talk."

"Oh, I don't know," Ellis responded. "Seems like you've done well up to now."

"If you're not going to tell me why my father hired you—"

"And I'm not."

"You can at least tell me if he said anything about me."

"Let's see. I believe the only mention of you was when he was introducing me to Emperado. Said you and the horse get along famously."

"He's fabulous, isn't he?"

"Well, he appeared fabulous to me… but then I don't know much about horses… or you for that matter. Why not tell me about yourself?"

"All right, since you asked," she said, taking another drink before continuing. "I'm the great man's daughter. To his everlasting chagrin. Always wanted a son. That's why even though my name is Alexis, he made sure everyone would call me Alex. Kind of sick, don't you think."

"Whoa. I thought it might take you a little longer to get into familial discontent. Either you don't handle your liquor very well or you have some serious daddy issues."

"Who wouldn't? With all he's done."

"Look. I don't know what he's done as it relates to you. All I know is that he's paying me to help with a matter I can't discuss. That's the way I do business."

"Did he tell you I have a son?"

"Now that you mention it, he did. Named Tanner, I think he said. Bit of a handful I bet. And where would the little fellow be right now while his mother is out drinking with a shady P. I.?"

"He's well taken care of. I told his nanny I'd be gone for a while. Are you questioning my parenting skills?"

"Not at all. Just engaging in some of that small talk you referred to earlier."

"Well I can assure you I'm a damn sight better parent than the one I have."

"Really? You seem to have turned out okay. I mean as far as I can tell in the hour or so since we've met."

"Well, that's not because of him, believe me. If there's anything about me that's remotely normal it's because of my mother."

"She passed on, right? A number of years ago? I think I read that somewhere when I was Googling your dad."

"I'm sure you probably did. He somehow managed to paper over that little bit of history."

"What do you mean," Ellis asked. "Died of heart failure, I read."

"That's right. Her heart failed when she turned the pistol around and blew a hole in it."

"Your mother committed suicide? That wasn't in any of the articles I went through."

"Of course it wasn't. He saw to that. Didn't want his reputation besmirched with such an ugly incident. But you can believe me. I'm the one who found her."

Ellis's tone immediately segued to genuine sympathy. "I'm sorry. That must have been awful for you."

"Not a picture that ever goes away, you know."

"Yeah, I do. I was in the military. Saw a number of things I'd rather forget. But you're right, it doesn't work that way."

She downed what was left of her drink. He followed suit.

"Can we get another?"

"Sure," he said. Then Ellis looked toward the bar and raised two fingers. Griff saw him right away. He had kept an eye on the couple for some time. She made it easy. After bringing the drinks and taking away the empties, he went back to refilling orders and watching from afar as the two went back to their conversation.

"Are you sure you can't tell me what my father has asked you to do?"

Ellis reached inside his coat pocket and pulled out the check he left with, keeping the side turned to him that showed how much it was for. "I've accepted a retainer. That means I keep a lid on it."

"What if I double what he's paying you?"

"You don't know what he's paying me."

"What if I double it anyway."

"You don't want to make that offer. And I don't want to accept it."

"Professional ethics?"

"Sounds like you think it's an oxymoron."

"You mean I've actually run across an honorable detective, shamus, private dick, whatever you want to call yourself?"

"That's for others to decide," he said, slipping the check back in his pocket. "But as I've repeatedly told you. I can't discuss what I'm doing for your father. Why don't you just ask him."

"We're currently not on speaking terms."

"Really? Why is that?"

She took another drink before not answering his question.

"Okay. You can't tell me what he hired you to do. But suppose I want to hire you."

"I'm going to be kind of busy for a while."

"What… you can't walk and chew gum at the same time… keep stepping on the wad you spit out. No wonder you guys are called gumshoes," she said, imbibing again.

Ellis wondered if she was getting tight. He decided she wasn't. The tear in her eye may have had something to do with his snap judgment.

"I want to hire you to help find my husband."

"Your husband? Is he missing? How long's he been gone?"

"Couple of weeks now."

"No contact? Notes, calls, anything like that?"

"Nothing."

"Ever happen before?"

"Never."

"No benders from time to time?"

"He drinks… but usually not that much."

"Sorry. Have to ask. Another woman?"

"No reason to think so."

"What'd the police say?"

"Haven't contacted them."

"Why is that?"

"My father didn't want them involved?"

"He give a reason?"

"My father doesn't explain himself to me. My guess is he doesn't want anyone to know."

"Because?"

"Because he probably had something to do with it."

Ellis took a drink of his own before saying, "What makes you think that?"

"My father loathes my husband. Thinks Gary's useless. Believes he only married me for our money. Even browbeat me into not changing my last name to Gary's when we wed. His name's Drexel. Gary Drexel."

"Why does your father feel that way about your husband?"

"Gary doesn't work. At least not now. He was a teacher when we got married, working on a doctoral thesis in the humanities."

"Let me guess. He's still working on it."

"My father offered him a job in one of his companies. Gary said he needed time to keep working on his thesis, so he turned him down. People don't turn my father down. I assume that check in your pocket verifies that."

"You should involve the police."

"I'd rather involve you."

"Like I said—"

"Look, you're an investigator. I want to hire you to investigate the disappearance of my husband. If my father hired you for the same thing, then you can turn me down. If he didn't… if it was for some other reason, then I can't see why you won't help me. What's your going rate? I'll pay it."

"It's already been paid," came the calm voice with the slight Irish lilt. Skeffington was standing beside the booth overlooking them both. Ellis wasn't sure how long he'd been doing so.

"The bill… for your drinks… I've already taken care of it," Skeffington said. "With the barman. Come Ms. Alex. I'll drive you home."

"Not sure the lady has finished her—"

"That's all right, Mr. Ellis, I do believe I've had enough. Thank you for the drinks… your time… and you're help."

"Look, if there's any question…" Ellis began, but Alex cut him short.

"I'll be fine, really. Mr. Skeffington's an excellent driver. We'll be back at the house in no time, won't we Mr. Skeffington?"

"Indeed we will, ma'am."

Ellis rose. "Good night, then. Very nice to have met you."

"And you," Alex said, offering her hand.

Bit odd, Ellis thought, but he reached out to shake her hand anyway and felt a card. He quickly placed his left hand over both of theirs and palmed it. She turned immediately and walked toward the entrance.

Skeffington, who had yet to follow, looked at Ellis's eyes, not his hand, and said, "I'd be wary, Mr. Ellis, of anything Ms. Alex has to say."

"Oh, why is that?"

"She's an inveterate liar."

CHAPTER 6

THE DRIVE FROM BENNY'S BACK to Ellis's apartment near Balboa Park was filled with cool air and cognitive dissonance. The card she had passed him simply read *A McC* with a phone number underneath. Ellis knew he'd be complicating things if he took Alex's request seriously, and even though he didn't think Skeffington noticed the hand-off, he knew the man's comment was less advice and more warning. The P.I. also assumed the task that McCullum had given him was not going to be as cut and dried as it sounded. Tasks from clients never were. Especially rich clients. Of course, he had never had a client as rich as C. Tyler McCullum, or for that matter, Alex McCullum. But if everything was easy, life would be exceedingly boring, he thought. So, at least for the moment, he figured he now had two clients.

After arriving at his apartment and taking his English Bulldog, Osgood, out for a necessary walk, he sat down at his computer and Googled Gary Drexel, San Diego. He got a few hits and head shots but nothing that seemed right to him. He jumped over to LinkedIn and tried that. Ten Gary Drexels showed up. Three in San Diego. One was listed as a professor. He brought up a picture. Promising, Ellis thought, guessing the fellow he was looking at was early to mid-thirties. He had hair longer than most guys wore it, a relatively unkempt beard, and the obligatory teacher's uniform—corduroy jacket with patches at the elbows. Ellis clicked on the photo, drug it to his desktop, then printed a couple of copies. On his way to bed, he rubbed Osgood's massive head and said, "Partner, what are we getting ourselves into?" The dog was noncommittal.

Morning found Ellis on his way downtown. He figured he'd wait to call Alex until he'd made the initial contact her father had asked him to make. The P. I. was a longtime advocate of first come, first served. Per C. Tyler McCullum's instructions, he was to meet with a man named Edward Broadhurst who was staying at The Guild, a chic boutique hotel in the middle of San Diego's business district. McCullum had been less than forthcoming about how he knew Broadhurst had access to the twelfth palomino. That was of no consequence, he had told Ellis. The P. I. was simply to represent himself as the emissary of an unknown potential buyer recommended by Dudley Graves, owner of one of the city's foremost art galleries. Ellis assumed that McCullum didn't want Graves handling the purchase alone in case the potential deal became less clandestine and more confrontational. A purveyor of art, while far more cultured, would likely prove a lot less capable than an ex-military man if the transaction went south and the proverbial excrement hit the wind machine.

Ellis pulled up in front of the hotel and left his keys with the valet. Entering the lobby, he found the mid-century modern vibe attractive, though he couldn't say as much for the dour clerk behind the counter.

"Hello. Do you have a Mr. Broadhurst staying here? Edward Broadhurst."

"We're not at liberty to provide information regarding our guests."

"I'm not really looking for information, I just want to make sure he's still here."

"Guest privacy is paramount at The Guild."

"I'm sure it is. But I need to know if he's here."

"And what is your name, sir?"

"My name is Brig Ellis. I have an appointment with Mr. Broadhurst."

Thin, manicured fingers clicked letters on a keyboard no more than a second and a half as the clerk said, "Ellis... Ellis... no, none of our guests have left word to expect a Mr. Ellis."

"Really? Perhaps that's because he assumed you'd just let him know someone was here to see him."

"Have you tried calling?"

"Pardon me," Ellis responded.

"Did it not occur to you that if you simply called the hotel, then asked for a guest named Broadhurst, that the operator would simply connect you."

"Actually, that hadn't occurred to me," Ellis said. "You know why?"

"No. Why?"

"Because I assumed that a hotel this classy would not entrust the front desk to a condescending twit."

Stung momentarily, but quickly rebounding, the clerk pointed to a phone bank on the left side of the lobby. "House phones are just a step away, sir."

"As might be comeuppance," Ellis countered, "if I were in less of a hurry this morning."

"Sticks and stones sir, sticks and stones. Have a nice day."

Ellis simply shook his head and walked to the phones where the operator did indeed put the call through. A voice answered, names were exchanged, and soon Ellis was on his way to the third floor. The door was answered after the second knock.

"Come in, Mr. Ellis."

The P.I. was ushered into a contemporary room with barren, white walls interrupted only by jet black window frames. The bed, desk, two chairs, a table, and a wall-mounted flat screen television were all extremely svelte.

Thin, metal legs supported the furniture, their design replicated as arm rests for the matching leather chairs. None of the chic furniture, however, gave any indication it would actually be capable of supporting the room's occupant.

In earlier, more gentile times, Broadhurst would have been referred to as portly. Today's woke society would probably call him stout. In point of fact, he was fat; his obesity was such that it could be said of his pinstriped suitcoat's button and its intended hole, that never the twain shall meet. The man tried to make up for it with a tie the length of an adolescent python. *Must have had them hand-made*, Ellis thought. Broadhurst was bald as a cue ball with brown eyebrows that matched a similarly muddy beard. Grown no doubt, Ellis mused, to camouflage a triple chin.

"Won't you sit down," Broadhurst asked, pointing to one of the black leather arm chairs.

"Ah, sure," Ellis replied, taking a seat and wondering how it would be humanly possible for Broadhurst to wedge his prodigious derrière into the remaining one.

"Care for a cup of coffee," the corpulent man asked, taking a drink from the cup he had already poured for himself. "Somewhat bitter this morning, actually. But I added a few sweeteners." Indeed, the multitude of yellow Splenda wrappers cluttered the tray like battlefield dead.

"No. I'll pass. Thanks anyway," Ellis said.

"Well, then…" Broadhurst began, his voice rumbling low and guttural, as if it came, perhaps appropriately, from a bear's cave. "I was told by Mr. Graves that a gentleman named Brig… intriguing forename… Ellis, would be coming to see me. I hope you don't mind my asking, but you can understand, certainly, why I might want to see some identification."

Ellis had picked up the hint of an accent initially, but it remained somewhat undefinable. Slightly British, or Canadian perhaps. He put the question on a back burner, assuming he wouldn't necessarily get a truthful answer anyway.

"No problem."

Pulling his wallet from his breast pocket. Ellis extracted his driver's license and was about to hand it to Broadhurst. He held it momentarily while the round one, pinky finger extended, partook of another drink of coffee. He then used a napkin to dab the facial hair surrounding his mouth, commenting again on the seemingly sour Brazilian blend. Then he took the I.D. Ellis was offering.

Looking back and forth from the license to the man, Broadhurst said, "Yes. Yes. Very good. You are at least whom you appear to be. But men in our profession must be careful, must we not?"

Ellis wasn't exactly sure what profession Broadhurst

was in, but he answered anyway.

"It always pays to be careful," the P.I. said, retrieving his I.D. from the man.

"Should we act as if we'd care to know more about one another, Mr. Ellis? Or would you rather... as you Americans are want to say... cut to the chase."

"I didn't really come to socialize," Brig answered.

"Nor do I expect you to," the rotund one said. "So, let us... what's the phrase... talk turkey."

"Or maybe horses."

"Ha. Ha. Horses. Indeed. Yes. Let's talk horses."

Ellis realized the moment had come. Broadhurst was actually going to attempt to sit down in the remaining empty chair. He watched in amazement as the man's protruding poundage slowly filled up the piece of furniture and spilled over the arms like a soufflé atop its ramekin.

"I understand you wish to acquire a certain miniature."

"Not me personally," Ellis said, "I'm representing a client who prefers to remain anonymous."

"Ah, yes. Your client. I see. And he... or perhaps she... is familiar with the item's origin?"

"Very familiar. Or I wouldn't be here."

"Of course. I only ask as a polite way of ascertaining whether your client is prepared to offer compensation that acknowledges the true value of the objet d'art under discussion."

"My client is not prepared to *offer* compensation," Ellis responded. "My client is prepared to hear the asking price."

Broadhurst took another sip of coffee, grimaced as he swallowed, then again dabbed his blobfish lips with a small napkin before saying, "Yes. A skilled negotiator, I see. Well, your client should understand that there is no *asking* price. There is only the *firm price* of five million dollars."

"Really," Ellis responded. Doing his best to sound surprised. "That seems inordinately high."

"Quality has its worth, Mr. Ellis. And I assure you this item is of the highest quality. And, since you say that your client is aware of its history, he… or she… must also be aware of the incredible challenges that have been involved over decades in tracking down and securing the palomino."

"The price will not come down?"

"Not one dollar."

"Then it must not go up, either."

Putting his hand over his heart, Broadhurst said, "I assure you, Mr. Ellis—" but before he could finish, an embarrassing burp escaped involuntarily. "Oh, I am so sorry. My profound apologies. It must be this appalling coffee, Anyway, as I was saying… my word is my bond. Five million dollars. No more. No less."

"It's my understanding," Ellis began, "that Dudley

Graves of Graves Art will authenticate at time of purchase."

"That is correct. Mr. Graves has agreed to authenticate the miniature, as well as hosting the sale. I have agreed to compensate him generously for his involvement."

Probably not as generously as McCullum may already have, Ellis thought to himself. "My client would like to complete this transaction as soon as possible. When can the sale take place?"

"If your client is agreeable, tomorrow night, ten p.m. at Mr. Grave's establishment. His close of business is eight o'clock. He asked that we enter via the rear of the gallery… to attract less attention. It probably goes without saying, but just so it is definitely understood… payment will need to be in cash. Can it be raised by then?"

"It can," Ellis answered. "By the way, do you have the miniature here? Would it be possible for me to see it?"

"Oh no, I don't have it with me. Never having met you before… well, I simply couldn't take a chance you know. But it's in a safe place. A very safe place."

"That's good, Mr. Broadhurst. Safety is important," Ellis said, rising. "Particularly when dealing with such valuable merchandise. So… I will see you at ten p.m. tomorrow night at Graves Art with the agreed upon compensation." Then Ellis pulled one side of his suit coat aside to reveal his shoulder-holstered Glock. "And I'll be playing it safe as well."

Not wanting the man to embarrass himself further, Ellis added, "Don't bother to get up, enjoy your coffee, I can see myself out. See you tomorrow night." Then turning to leave, he said, "Good-bye."

Upon reaching the door, he had heard no response. Odd, Ellis thought. When you tell someone good-bye, there's always a response. The P.I. said again, "Good-bye Mr. Broadhurst, see you tomorrow night."

Again, nothing.

Ellis took his hand off the door knob, turned, and walked back to Broadhurst. He was still seated in the chair, eyes open, staring at the wall in front of him, or perhaps at eternity.

"Mr. Broadhurst? Mr. Broadhurst," Ellis said, lightly shaking his shoulder. The slight jostle was enough to send both the recipient, and the chair in which he was stuffed, crashing to the floor.

Ellis knelt down and used two fingers to find the man's carotid artery. He soon realized there was no pulse. There was only a bald, bearded fat man dead on the floor, with foam at his mouth and a chic Euro-centric chair clamped to his colossal backside.

CHAPTER 7

THE PHONE RANG ONLY ONCE before it was answered.

"This is Detective Ramirez."

"Walter, this is Brig Ellis."

"Hey Brig, what's shaking?"

"Actually, it's what's not shaking that I'm calling about. I'm at The Guild Hotel and—"

"The Guild. Coming up in the world, huh?"

"This is not about my status, Walter. It's something a bit more serious."

"Okay. I'm all ears."

"As I said, I'm at The Guild, room 318, and I'm not alone. There's a stiff here."

"You mean a really boring guy… or a body?"

"The latter."

"You have anything to do with his current condition?"

"Nothing. But the desk clerk knows I came up. My finger prints are here and there in the room. And my car's in their garage. Figured there was no point in putting off the inevitable. That's why I called you."

"Got a read on cause of death?"

"I'm no expert, but my bet's poison."

"Really? Don't get a lot of that these days. You probably don't need me to tell you this but stay where you are. Don't touch anything in the room that you haven't touched already. I'll be there in a few minutes with some of the crime scene crew."

Ellis had known Walter Ramirez for a long time. Like the P. I., he had been in the army and the two met in jump school. While airborne assaults were no longer standard operating procedure for getting troops from safe areas to a battle zone, parachuting still served a useful purpose when wanting to get someone behind enemy lines clandestinely. And in typical military thinking, training men en masse was a lot more efficient than individual instruction.

There's nothing that tends to bond people together more than jumping out of a perfectly good airplane. Before that happened for Ellis and Ramirez however, there was a lot of physical and mental training that preceded it. Training that generated camaraderie, fatigue, and fear. Fatigue in the form of five mile runs with full gear to simulate getting to one's objective in a hurry. Fear in actually getting one's ass out the airplane door at twelve hundred feet above the ground. The two men wound up experiencing both as they lived in the same barracks, were assigned to the same squad, and were lined up next to each other for the full three weeks of training. Like many others before them, they made a pact. If either one ever froze in the door, the other would send a swift kick of his government issue combat boot into the butt of the hesitator. Neither ever had to do that. They did however, have to do something no one ever wants to do.

On the last jump of the last day of training, their squad was boarded differently than before. Rather than being in front of and/or behind each other, the two wound up on opposite sides of the C130 as it rose into the sky. Once they reached the drop zone and the green light came on, soldiers began jumping from each door. Their exits were supposed to be staggered, so the prop wash wouldn't blow two jumpers into each other. But speed, excitement, and adrenaline, often alter the best laid plans of mice, men, and the military. Both men jumped from their respective sides simultaneously. The force of the engines blew them backward and they slammed into one another like two rams butting horns. Ramirez's arm got caught in Ellis's strap. The latter's chute began to deploy, but the former's didn't.

Ramirez frantically wrapped his arms around his squad mate's waist as his own silk fluttered but never caught enough air to open. The two men were coming down on one chute. Their descent was discernibly faster than the other jumpers they were dropping past. Ellis was trying to guide his parachute with one hand and hold onto Ramirez with the other. Mother earth was coming up fast. Ellis looked down at the man hanging onto him for dear life and shouted, "Fall to my right when we hit. I'll go left." The words preceded touch down by less than seconds. They hit and fell in opposite directions. Ellis was being pulled away by ground-wind until he hit his quick release snap that collapsed his chute. He scrambled free and ran back to check on Ramirez who was lying face down. When Ellis turned him over, his friend's eyes were wide open. He seemed to be all in one piece and okay, except the legs of his fatigue pants were soaking wet. Ramirez quickly blurted, "Just tell them I landed in water, okay?"

After jump school, each returned to their respective units and neither man saw the other until years later. Both were California natives, but neither knew the other was living and working in San Diego until one day when they happened to run into each other at a burrito stand near the beach. Not surprisingly, their first topic of conversation was their duet drop. Ramirez said he more than owed Ellis for holding onto him all the way down. So Ellis suggested the cop pay for the burritos.

The P. I.'s job as a private dick occasionally brought him in contact with the San Diego Police Department. When that happened, Ramirez always did what he could to help. In addition to a friendship forged over a thousand feet in the air, he didn't view private investigators as one size fits all, the way most of the other cops in his division did. Ellis was certainly the reason.

When he called his old pal, the P.I. knew Ramirez wouldn't give him a pass on a dead body in a high profile hotel, but he also knew he wouldn't be subjected to a trip to the station, hours of questioning, and threats of losing his license, either. There were benefits to having a friend on the force.

While he was waiting for the police to arrive, Ellis took a look around the room. He didn't have gloves with him, so he used the bottom of his suit coat to keep his fingers covered as he opened the closet. A couple of suits were hanging there. He rummaged through the pockets not really expecting to find anything and he didn't. In the bathroom he saw typical traveling incidentals on the sink along with a leather case for carrying them. To look in the case without leaving his prints, he pulled off a bit of toilet paper. Nothing there either. He used his elbow to flush the toilet paper. In the time Ellis had left before the calvary arrived he decided to make another call. Pulling out the card Alex had slipped him the night before, he punched the numbers into his cell phone.

"Hello. Who is calling?"

"That's an odd way to answer the phone."

"Who is this?"

"Forgotten my voice already, huh? Must not have made much of an impression."

"Is this you… Mr. Ellis… the…"

"The private investigator you were having drinks with last night."

Concern in her voice, she avoided his answer and asked immediately, "Do you think Skeffington saw me pass you the card?"

"I don't think so. Does it matter?"

"Are you going to help find my husband?"

"I've decided to look into it. I'll ask around. Check a few things out."

"And you won't mention anything about this to my father?"

"Fair's fair. Since I won't tell you what I'm doing for him, I won't tell him what I'm doing for you. Until you're ready for me to do so."

"Thank you. Should we discuss your fee?"

"There's no discussion. The fee's two hundred dollars a day for at least a week. At the end of the week we can decide if either of us wants to extend."

"That's a lot less than I thought it would be."

"I reserve the right to let you know if I have to increase it."

"What might cause that?"

"Unforeseen circumstances."

"Such as?"

"Circumstances I can't foresee."

"That certainly clears things up."

"No increases unless I clear them with you in advance."

"Agreed. Is there anything I can do to help?"

"Go to LinkedIn.com. Type in Gary Drexel San Diego. If one of the guys there is your husband, call me back and let me know if the picture of him is relatively current. You can see my number on your phone, right?"

"Yes."

"If I don't answer, just leave a message. I'll probably be with some people when you call."

"Okay, I've got it."

"By the way, have you ever heard your father, or anyone else for that matter, mention a man named Broadhurst… Edward Broadhurst?"

"I… don't think so. Broadhurst. No I can't recall hearing that name before."

The voice came from the other side of the door. "Brig… you in there?"

"Gotta go now, Alex. Talk to you later."

Ellis ended the call before she had a chance to respond. Then yelled, "That you Ramirez? Yeah, come on in."

The latch turned, and the door, which Broadhurst never re-locked after letting Ellis in, swung slowly inward. No one was standing in the opening. Again came Ramirez's voice, "Nothing funny going on in there, right Brig?"

"Nobody's laughing in here, Walter. Come see for yourself."

The police detective who had been up against the wall outside the door, stepped into the opening. He looked from Ellis to the floor, where it was impossible to miss the beached whale.

"Guy looks dead," Ramirez remarked.

"Guess that's why you made detective, Walter, your keen powers of observation."

Turning to the CSI crew behind him, Ramirez said, "Give me a minute guys." Then pulled the door shut behind him as he walked into the room.

"Got an explanation for this, Brig?"

"Man drank too much coffee. Apparently killed him."

"I'll need more than that."

"We were having a chat. He was drinking coffee. Offered me one. Can't believe I turned it down. Conversation ended. I get up to leave, walk to the door to say good-bye. No response. I turn back to see why not and the guy's stone dead. I get on the phone and called you."

"Use the phone in the room?"

"No, my cell phone."

"You didn't say you heard him fall over when you were at the door."

"That's because he hadn't fallen. I went back to him, couldn't get him to respond. I tapped him on the shoulder and… I don't know, maybe I shook him a little too much, and the chair went over with him in it."

"How'd you ascertain he was dead?"

"Checked for a pulse. Couldn't find one. Assumed he was kaput."

"Make any sounds? Like choking, or gurgling, or gasping for breath?"

"None. I guess it's possible that it could have been a stroke or a heart attack or something like that. I mean look at the guy. His blood pressure was probably higher than the national debt."

"A minute ago, you said 'conversation ended.' What was the conversation about?"

"Art."

"Not funny."

"Not meant to be."

"Who was he? What's your connection to him?"

"His name, I assume, is Edward Broadhurst. That's the sum total of what I know about the guy. I was only here to see if he had located some art a client of mine is interested in."

"Who's the client?"

"That's confidential."

"This is a potential homicide."

"When it becomes less potential and more actual, then we can talk."

"I could take you in, you know?"

"I know. And I could have left without calling you. But did I?"

"You touch anything else in the room?"

"Do I look like a toucher?"

"So," Ramirez asked, "had he located it or not?"

"Located what?"

"The art you said your client… the one you haven't named yet… is supposedly interested in."

"We didn't get that far," Ellis lied. "He was playing coy. I was playing pissed off and leaving. Negotiating tactics, you know. Then it happened like I told you."

Ramirez asked, but his interrogative was more statement than question. "You'll be available if I need to get hold of you, right?"

"I will Walter, and thanks for not keeping me here all day," Ellis said sincerely. "I appreciate it."

Ramirez crossed to the door, opened it, and said to the crew waiting in the hall, "Come on in fellows, Mr. Ellis is just leaving."

CHAPTER 8

ELLIS WASN'T IN THE HABIT of lying to friends, and that's what he considered Ramirez. But CONFIDENTIAL MATTERS stamped on his business card meant what it said. So he was definitely less than truthful when he recounted what he and Broadhurst talked about. Ellis was committed to keeping McCullum's name out of things until he knew more, and right now there was a lot he didn't know. Regardless of what the fat man said, Ellis didn't know if Broadhurst had really secured the palomino. If he did, Ellis didn't know where it was. He didn't know positively, whether the man had been poisoned or not? And if he had been, Ellis didn't know who might be involved, what the particular motive was, and whether or not he had just been in the wrong place at the wrong time or whether he had in fact, been set up. But why would anyone want or need to do that? As the elevator doors opened and Ellis stepped out he did know one thing. The lovely brunette behind the desk was a lot more pleasant to look at than the irritating fellow who gave him a hard time earlier. Ellis couldn't help himself.

"Shift change, huh?"

The brunette responded, "Sorry? Can I help you sir?"

"You've helped me already by being much more accommodating than your coworker who was here earlier."

"Ah, sorry again, but I've been on the desk all morning."

"Well, not *all* morning surely, because when I came in earlier, the individual behind the counter was definitely not you. He didn't look like you. He didn't talk like you. And he definitely wasn't as nice as you."

"Sir, there must be some mistake," she said, looking down at a printout beside the computer terminal. "None of our male associates are scheduled to be on this desk today, either before or after me. And as I said, I've been here… oh, wait a minute, I remember now." She looked at Ellis rather sheepishly. "You know sir, there was just once this morning when I had to excuse myself and run to the ladies' room. But I asked my supervisor, Madge, to fill in while I was gone."

"I doubt that this individual was called Madge."

"Well, one second. Let's see." She quickly turned from the counter, took a couple of steps and stuck her head in an office that was behind her and to the left. Ellis heard her say, "Madge, can you join us for a moment? There's a gentleman needing help."

Ellis had only stopped on his way out to do a little flirting, but now his curiosity was piqued. By the time the young woman returned to the counter, an older woman stepped out of the office. She was tall, somewhere in the vicinity of forty, and also remarkably pleasant. "How can I help?"

The young woman spoke before Ellis could answer. "Madge, you remember this morning when I had to run to the powder room and I asked if you could watch the desk for me?"

"Yes, I recall," Madge said

"Well, apparently this gentleman came to the desk and he thought a male was manning the counter then. I've told him no men are scheduled for the desk today. Perhaps you—"

If there had been a light bulb over Madge's head, it would have come on at that moment. She cut in and said, "Oh, Jean, I just remembered. I'm so embarrassed. Right after you asked me if I could cover the desk for a moment and I said, yes, certainly... well, the telephone rang and I answered it. Mr. Landers wanted information from the personnel... I mean human resource files, and I got so involved that I forgot to come out and watch the counter until you returned." Turning to Ellis, she said, "Perhaps that was why there was no one here when you came over."

"Well, you see that's just it," Ellis said. "There was someone here and he was definitely—"

Shouts cut him off. "Ms. Stanton! Ms. Stanton!" They

came from a short man in white work clothes and an apron who was sprinting toward the three of them. The apparent kitchen worker was yelling as he ran. "Ms. Stanton. Call the police! Call the police!"

Madge responded. "Juan, calm down. Speak slowly. What's the matter? Why should I call the police?"

Juan didn't calm down, nor did he reduce the speed of his delivery. "It's the dumpster behind the hotel. The dumpster!"

"What's the matter with the dumpster," Madge asked.

"There's a man in it. A man. I think he's dead! We must call the police."

"You're in luck," Ellis said. "The police are already here."

Surprised, Madge said, "They are?"

"They are," Ellis quickly replied

"I was not informed," Madge said.

"They can be lax about protocol," Ellis replied, "And when they want to be, they can be quite unobtrusive." Pulling out his cell phone, he told the three, "I'll call the officer in charge. He's upstairs. I'm sure he'll be right here. We should probably all stay where we are until he comes down."

"Oh, this is so dreadful," the pretty brunette said. "Thank you so much for helping Mr... ."

"Ellis. Brig Ellis."

"While we wait, Mr. Ellis, would you like a cup of coffee?"

"Absolutely not," Ellis barked involuntarily. "No coffee for anyone."

~ ~ ~ ~ ~

They had been in the alley behind the hotel for half an hour. Ellis, Ramirez, Juan, and the dead man. Of course, the dead man had been there longer. How much longer was part of the subject of their conversation. Juan had explained how he came out to dump the remains of the morning breakfast service and found the body. Ellis had explained how the lifeless body in the dumpster had previously not been lifeless and had given him a hard time when he arrived and asked for Broadhurst. Ramirez had explained, on his cell phone to the precinct, that he now had two crime scenes and needed an additional CSI team. The dead man volunteered nothing. He was now beyond having to explain anything to anyone.

Ramirez let Juan return to work, but told him not to leave before the incoming CSI team arrived. The policeman wanted the cook's fingerprints. He assumed they were on the dumpster and he didn't want time wasted getting the cook's digits confused with the killer's. Both Ramirez and Ellis concluded there had, in fact, been a killing because of the bullet hole entry at the base of the dead man's skull. Plus the sizable exit wound in his forehead. Suicide as a manner of death was quickly discarded by both men as the deceased would have had to be an incredible contortionist to shoot himself in the back of his head and then leap into the trash receptacle, which was taller that he was. Not all detective work is rocket science.

The two men then turned from what they knew to what they thought; a conversation filled both with questions and conjecture.

"So… what's the connection between this body and the one on the third floor," Ramirez asked.

Ellis answered with a question. "Convinced there's a connection?"

"I stopped believing in coincidence a long time ago. One hotel. Two bodies. Time of death's probably going to show they didn't die that many minutes apart. What do you think?"

"I think," Ellis began, "two dead guys are not the only things weird around here. There are also a lot of unanswered questions. Like who the hell is the guy in the dumpster? Yes, he's wearing a hotel uniform, but the cook didn't know him, and I'm willing to bet the two women at the desk don't know him either. What was he doing here? Why was he behind the desk when I came in? Maybe he slipped back there when the brunette went to the toilet. Maybe he doctored the coffee that was delivered to Broadhurst. Maybe he didn't do what he did by himself.

And maybe, when he was about to leave the scene, his partner, or partners in crime, decided to leave him behind permanently."

"Why would they do that?"

"I don't have any idea. I'm not getting paid to come up with answers to any of this. You are. I'm just one of the tax payers footing your bill."

"And I'm wondering if your presence here is not a coincidence either?"

"That kind of wondering will only cloud your mind," Ellis responded. "Stay focused on tried and true police work. I'll leave you to it."

"Okay, but don't—"

"I know. Don't take any long out-of-town trips. No plans to do so."

Ellis was about to walk away when he remembered what he had in his suit pocket. He pulled it out and handed it to Ramirez saying, "Say, Walter, do me a favor, will you? Can you show this picture to the guys at the morgue and see if he happened to have checked in recently?"

"Who the hell is this?"

"Name's Gary Drexel."

"And you don't know if he's dead or alive… or you don't know where the body happens to be?"

"I'm hoping he's not dead, but I'm exploring the possibility for a client?"

"Which you don't want to disclose at the moment."

"Right. But if harm has come to him, I'll let you know what I know."

"That's big of you."

"You're a mensch, Walter. Don't let anyone tell you you're not."

CHAPTER 9

AS HE WAS WAITING FOR the valet to bring his car around, Ellis remembered that old scripture about idle hands being the devil's workshop. Seemed to him there were too many devilish things going on already so he pulled out his phone to make a call. When he did, he saw that Alex had left a message. She confirmed that the photo of her husband was relatively recent and he did still look much the same. Good, he thought. Then he put a call in to McCullum to bring him up to speed on the morning's activities. Skeffington answered.

"McCullum residence."

Ellis recognized the voice. "Hey, Skeffington, this is Brig Ellis. I need to talk to your boss."

"I can convey whatever message you might have."

"Actually, you can't. Because I'm not going to tell you why I'm calling. He's my client. You're not. So, just let me talk to him."

There was a pause that pregnant wouldn't cover, then came the reply, "Please hold... for as long as it takes."

Damn, thought Ellis, *I pissed him off. Now he's going to take his sweet time getting the big guy on the phone.*

Ellis was right. It was a good two minutes before McCullum came on the line. An eternity it seemed. Long enough to actually make him wish for some sort of inane elevator music to occupy his time. The P. I. made a mental note not to let Skeffington's attitude bug him so much.

"McCullum here. Are you there, Mr. Ellis?"

"I am. Wanted to let you know there's been a bit of a wrinkle in what you asked me to do."

"I'm listening."

"This fellow, Broadhurst, you asked me to meet. Well I met him, but now he's dead."

"Are you in any way responsible for that?"

"No sir. Think he was poisoned before we connected. Apparently it just took a while to kick in, so I did get some information."

"Which is?"

"Well, as you thought, he was asking five million for the palomino. Asked if the cash could be available for a meet at Graves Art tomorrow night, ten o'clock."

"Does Dudley Graves know Broadhurst is dead?"

"Don't see how he could. Only happened a little over an hour ago. You think this Graves fellow had anything to do with it?"

"Like most wealthy people in San Diego, I've known

of Graves for some time. He often moves expensive art. Though he's not always the recipient of the price. Often he simply takes a fee for his involvement. A bit like keeping the crumbs that spill as a piece of cake is passed from one person to another."

"Broadhurst indicated that was the plan… said he was covering Grave's end. I assume the guy was putting money in both his pockets?"

"What do you mean," McCullum asked.

"He was getting a cut from Broadhurst for playing middle man, and I assume, something from you for keeping your involvement secret… to keep Broadhurst from driving the price up even more."

"My previous involvements with Graves would lead me to believe that he would not be averse to multiple income streams."

"Maybe he's not averse to padding his profits either."

"How so?"

"Well, if he knows where the palomino is, maybe he eliminates Broadhurst, accepts your money from me for the miniature, and keeps the five mil for himself. Plus whatever you've already paid him."

"In my opinion, Mr. Ellis, Dudley Graves is not the type to traffic in murder. He's the sort of fellow who has the laundry starch his skivvies as well as his shirts."

"Wouldn't necessarily have to get his own hands dirty.

Particularly if he had an accomplice. You ever see a guy at his place... thin, glasses, balding... manicured nails?"

"I've never been inside Graves Art, Mr. Ellis. Shopkeepers come to me. But why do you ask about this other man?"

"Because he gave me heat on the way in the hotel. Apparently, he didn't actually work there. And his body was found in a dumpster behind the place. Pretty much intact except for the bullet hole in his head."

"Are the police involved? How much do they know?"

"I called them about Broadhurst. Had to. My prints were all over the place. But I've been able to keep your name out of it... so far."

"Continue to do that, Mr. Ellis. That's one of the things you're being paid for... confidentiality."

"Not sure I can keep a lid on it if bodies keep turning up. But I'll do what I can."

"What do you propose for a next step?"

"You don't happen to have five million in cash stuffed in a sock drawer, do you?"

"As it happens, I do. That and more, actually. Rainy day fund, you know."

"I think we should move forward as if the deal that I discussed with Broadhurst is still on. That means I'll need the money to make the buy. If possible, I'd like to come out to your place and pick it up this afternoon."

"I won't be here. Have a meeting scheduled out of town.

But I can have it ready for you to pick up. Some people might worry about handing over that much money to someone they don't really know that well. Might be concerned the individual would just take off with it and they'd never see the person or the cash again. But I don't think that's the case with you, Mr. Ellis, because having looked into your background and having met you, I think you're an honest man. I also think you probably know that there's no place on this planet where you could go and hide that a man of my means couldn't find you."

"I appreciate your opinion… and your capabilities."

"We should forge ahead then."

"Good," Ellis began. "I'll come get the money and show up with it at Graves' place tomorrow night for the meeting Broadhurst suggested. If Graves isn't involved in Broadhurst's death, chances are he won't find out about it before then. My bet is that Broadhurst already had the miniature stowed away with Graves for safe keeping… just in case I was going to be more intimidating than facilitating."

"And you believe Graves will complete the sale without Broadhurst being there?"

"He will when I tell him that Broadhurst is now in the morgue. He'll realize his cut just went from whatever percent, to one hundred percent."

"And I assume that you assume he won't try any

shenanigans, because he knows the money's coming from me."

"Right. Since you were okay with him authenticating the miniature, I assume that he'll assume you're okay with paying him for the palomino as well. The fact that he won't have to share it with Broadhurst is irrelevant to you… I assume."

"Pardon my French, Mr. Ellis, but that's a lot of fucking assumptions."

"Disagree with any of them?"

"Not at the moment. But what if your other hypothetical is also correct?"

"Which one," Ellis asked. "I've lost count."

"What if Graves *was* involved with Broadhurst's death. There's always the chance he's more dangerous than he appears."

"Could be, Mr. McCullum. But then, so am I."

The phone call ended and the valet arrived with the P. I.'s car. Ellis tipped him, and after accepting the gratuity, the young man complimented the German classic. Ellis thanked him and responded, saying, "Timeless over trendy. You know."

"Yeah," the valet said. "Timeless over trendy. I'll remember that."

And probably use it too. Maybe the generation gap isn't as wide as advertised, Ellis wanted to believe, but really didn't. Before pulling away from the hotel and back onto the street, he decided to make one more call.

"Hello, who is this?"

"You really need to work on that greeting."

"It's you? Ellis, right?"

"Yes, Alex it's me. I'm flattered you now recognize my voice. But not my phone number, huh?"

"I've never been able to remember numbers."

"Well, I guess when there are so many in your bank account, that would be difficult."

"Why are you calling? Have you found something out about Gary?"

"No. I was just calling you back to thank you for letting me know that the picture does indeed look like him."

"So, you haven't done anything in regard to finding him?"

"I have a contact at the police department that I've asked to look into it. He may be able to provide information we don't have." Ellis didn't see the need to be specific about where he asked Ramirez to check. No point in heightening her concern unduly, he thought. But that wasn't the only thing he was thinking about.

"By the way, I'm coming out to your place this afternoon to pick up something. I understand your father's going to be away. Any chance we can talk? I'd like to hear more about why you think he might know more about your husband's disappearance than you do."

"I've got a dressage session at two o'clock."

"With the big palomino?"

"Emperado."

"That's right. Emperado. Can I watch you and your horse workout?"

"Can you stay quiet while you do?"

"As the proverbial mouse."

"Mice sometimes startle horses."

"I haven't startled a horse in a long time."

"We'll talk after, then."

"See you in the saddle."

CHAPTER 10

MCCULLUM HAD TOLD SKEFFINGTON THAT Ellis would be coming to the mansion. The jack-of-all-trades was also told to provide the P.I. with the money and have him sign a prepared receipt. When Ellis arrived, Skeffington met him at the door with an exceedingly heavy U. S. Army duffel bag. The weight of the bag was due to the enormous amount of cash that had been stuffed inside it. Outside it, on a clipboard that Skeffington handed Ellis to sign, was a receipt for five million dollars. "Mr. McCullum said you may count the money before signing, if you wish."

"Did you count it?"

"I did."

"How much is there?"

"Five million dollars."

"Were you asked to sign a receipt?"

"I'm a trusted employee."

"At the moment, I'm an employee."

"Surely the difference doesn't escape you."

"How long do you think it would take to count it?"

"At minimum, one hour."

"Can I peek in the bag," Ellis asked.

Skeffington pulled the zipper halfway down. Ellis looked inside at the most cash he'd ever seen in one place in his lifetime.

"If McCullum trusts you, I trust you, Skeffington. Here's my John Henry," the P. I. said, handing the clipboard back with the signed receipt. He then hoisted the duffel bag, walked to his car, opened his trunk, and with some degree of difficulty, stuffed it in. After closing and locking the trunk lid, he went back to the front door where Skeffington continued to stand.

"Uh, Alex… Ms. McCullum, invited me to watch her dressage session."

"She informed me. It's already underway in the corral behind the stable. I believe you know where that is."

"I do. Mr. McCullum showed it to me when I was here before. I'll just walk back, okay?"

"That will be fine," Skeffington said, starting to shut the door.

"Uh," Ellis interjected, "It would be shorter to just go directly through the house, wouldn't it?"

"Yes. It would," Skeffington said, closing the door in the P. I.'s face.

~ ~ ~ ~ ~

After walking around the mansion and continuing toward the stable, Ellis was having a hard time getting over Skeffington's unnecessary rudeness and superior attitude… and prissy personality… and whatever the hell it was that made the P.I. want to poke him in the throat to let the air out of his haughtiness. *Geez,* Ellis thought. *What a creep.* But his negative mental state segued into positivity when Alex and Emperado came into view.

She sat the horse like a pro, and dressed the part from head to foot. With her dark carbon helmet, black show jacket, white turtle neck, tan riding breeches and tall dressage boots, she looked like one of those rich women who graced the pages of publications such as *Equus* or *Horse & Rider. Of course,* Ellis thought to himself, *she was one, wasn't she?*

Emperado seemed even more regal than when Ellis saw him the first time. The stallion moved as one with its rider. Coordination between the animal and the woman in the saddle shone like a synchronistic ballet. It appeared as if the horse was making every move of his own accord, accepting the bit without the slightest tension or resistance. Emperado's pace and bearing looked effortless whether cantering, trotting, walking, or simply coming to a halt and standing obediently motionless. With his head held proudly erect, the great beast appeared as noble as the graceful beauty astride him. Ellis was appropriately impressed with both.

When the session was finished, Alex dismounted and broke the formalities that surrounded their workout. She put both of her hands on Emperado's muzzle. He lowered his head so she could put her cheek against it and give him a kiss. He was then handed over to a stable hand to take away for his rub down. Alex saw Ellis standing near the fence. She walked toward him and as she did she removed her riding helmet. Shaking her head, her red locks tumbled to her shoulders and for just a moment Ellis had to remind himself that she was not only a client, but a married one as well. At least as far as he knew… at this point in time.

Alex gestured toward a campaign table with two folding chairs that had been set up near the entrance to the stable. It was topped with two tumblers beside two bottles of liquor, one bourbon, one scotch. The P. I. felt complimented that she remembered his drink from the night before. A rush of temporary gentility washed over him and he pulled out one of the chairs for her to sit down.

"I like a whiskey after Emperado and I work out. It always feels like I've accomplished something."

Ellis took the liberty of pouring a drink for each of them. "Here's to horse and rider," he said.

"I'll drink to the horse part of that," she replied. And they both did.

"It's amazing how such a huge… and I assume, strong-willed animal… can be so responsive to what you want him to do."

"He's not that way with everyone, you know."

"Yes. Your father mentioned that you two have quite a bond."

"He did?"

"He did."

"Sorry. Just not used to hearing that my father paid me a compliment."

"Perhaps he compliments you more than you know. Compliments *about* you rather than to you."

"That would be his way. When one compliments his offspring, he's really complimenting himself, isn't he? You know… the parent actually being responsible for the child's accomplishment."

"If you say so. Frankly that's way too psychological for me."

"Years of therapy makes you think you're an expert. Even if you're just the patient."

"I wouldn't know," Ellis said. "Never tried it."

"Afraid of learning about yourself?"

"No. Afraid I'd just be paying someone to make me feel better… even when I shouldn't."

"Are there times we shouldn't feel better?"

"I've had lots of them."

"Like to wallow in self-pity, do you?"

"No. I just feel there's worth in occasional sadness, regret, even sorrow."

"Wow. Who's being psychological now?"

"Sorry," the P.I. said with a smile. "It won't happen again."

Each decided to have one more drink, but not more than one since Ellis had to drive back to the city and Alex said that she didn't want to seem tipsy around her son later. As it turned out, their conversation kept them from emptying their glasses anyway.

"Before Skeffington interrupted our last little talk last night, you said your father didn't care for your husband and may have even had something to do with his disappearance. Why did you say that?"

"He thinks Gary stole from him."

"Stole what?"

"A horse. A miniature horse."

Well, Ellis thought to himself, *this certainly muddies the water.*

"A miniature horse?"

"Yes. My father didn't tell you about them?"

"Like I said, I can't talk about anything your father and I might have discussed."

"I can't believe he didn't mention them. He seems to drone on about them to anyone new who comes to the house. Oh well, here's the short version."

Ellis let her go back over the miniatures' history. Thankfully, she truncated it much more than her father had.

"Anyway, my father thinks Gary swiped one when he took off. To sell on the black market, or wherever one sells things like that. I can't see him doing it, but—"

Playing along, Ellis interjected, "How many horses are there?"

"There are ten now. There were eleven. There's supposed to be an even dozen. I can't tell you how long my father's been looking for that twelfth one."

Ellis's internal random access memory quickly pulled up what McCullum had said to him. *"The fact is, the eleventh is virtually within my grasp."*

"You don't really think your father would harm your husband to get it back, do you?"

"My father would do whatever it takes to get it back. He wouldn't hesitate to harm Gary if the poor schmuck did take it. He'd just make sure I'd never know anything about it."

Ellis noted the way Alex referred to her husband. "I'm getting the impression that things between you and Gary may not have been idyllic before he disappeared."

Alex signed heavily before responding. When she did, it was with an obvious measure of chagrin. "The truth Mr. Ellis, is that Gary and I hadn't... I believe the polite phrase is 'gotten along' for quite some time. It pains me enormously to say this, but it seems that my father's opinion of Gary is probably closer to reality that my own. Gary's a weak man, Mr. Ellis. Selfish too. Looking back on it, I think maybe I married him because he seemed the opposite of my father... quiet, subdued... charming. That's what I saw on the outside. What I didn't see on the inside was the resentfulness."

"Resentful of what," Ellis asked.

"Oh, you know. Resentful of the rich. Bitter that people like my father, even people like me I suppose, had so much when individuals like him seemed to have so little in comparison."

"Liked to compare things, did he?"

"Oh yes. He was always comparing my father's conservative politics to his liberal views. Taking issue with the fact that, in his words, I probably have more pairs of shoes than one could find in most small countries. Belittling the fact that I spend time with a horse rather than the homeless."

"Did he practice what he preached?"

"Of course not. I'm not sure what he did before, but after we were married, he spent most of his time wasting it. Acting like he was working on his doctoral when he was actually doing little of anything other than haranguing everyone and occasionally drinking to excess. If you really want to know, I think Gary had come to hate himself as much as the things he hated. I think he felt that he had become as useless as the rest of us moneyed yet unworthy aristocrats. Maybe his ennui finally overwhelmed him."

"Excuse my lack of subtlety but the man had a hot wife and a young son. What kind of guy walks away from that?"

"I'm afraid our romantic life ended pretty much when Tanner was born. Probably as much my fault as his. I'm sure I lavished much more time and attention on my child than I did on my husband. Guess he got tired of that. Know he got tired of me. And I have to admit… the feeling became somewhat mutual."

"Then why do you want to find him?"

"Because he's the father of my son. Because I probably had as much to do with screwing up his life as he did. Because… while he is an unreliable, irresponsible asshole… and maybe even a thief… he's still a human being who doesn't deserve what might happen to him if my father finds him first. And because I couldn't live with myself if I didn't at least make a real effort to find and help him."

"That says as much about you as it does him. Is there still love involved?"

"Not really. But I can't help feeling that in many ways I'm responsible."

"Appreciate your honesty," Ellis said. Then added, "By the way, I like people who accept responsibility… whether they should or not."

CHAPTER 11

THE TREE-LINED SHADOWS OF A dying day were falling across the road as Ellis made his way back to the main highway. His morning had been bad enough, chatting up not just one man but two who quickly turned dead. His afternoon had moved from potentially pleasing to perplexing. He had taken on Alex's task while doing one for her father against his better judgment. Dumb, he told himself. But the simple truth was he liked being around her. She was smart, attractive, and concerned about someone she really had little reason to still be concerned about. You don't run into people like that every day, he mused, especially ones so lovely. But now, potential complications were rising exponentially.

Alex's missing person's case was crossing over into stolen property territory. Her father was obviously on Gary's trail, but apparently with a totally different outcome in mind from his daughter's. For McCullum to complete his palomino collection, he'd have to get the eleventh one back while Ellis secured the twelfth. But now the P. I. might be doing business not simply with an art dealer, but maybe a killer as well. Alex didn't want her father to know what she was up to and McCullum didn't want the police or anyone else to know what he was up to. Ellis's cop pal, Ramirez, was eventually going to demand to know what Ellis was up to. For an individual who was never a big fan of complexity, Ellis felt himself up to his eyeballs in it. Then his phone rang. Ellis recognized the number and pulled onto the shoulder of the road to stop and take the call.

"Hey, Ramirez, I was just thinking about you."

"Thinking that you ought to be telling me more than you have?"

"Not exactly. But you called me. What's up?"

"The picture of that dude that you gave me… the one to show the guys in the morgue."

"Yeah."

"Well, he wasn't one of their current residents."

"Oh."

"You sound disappointed."

"No. No. Just processing your input."

"Well, here's some more to process. While he wasn't one of the stiffs there, his wallet was recovered from a body that was brought in yesterday. Yep. Guy had been garroted. Body found near the harbor. When they checked him into the ice house, he had two wallets. His own… which had his picture and address on a Mexican driver's license… and the billfold of the guy you asked me to look into.

"What was the name of the guy who got his neck wrung?"

"You gonna tell me what you know about him?"

"*If* I know him, I'll tell you."

"Victor Fuentez. Tijuana address."

"Never heard of him. What's the address?"

"If you never heard of him, why do you care?"

"Just interested, you know."

"Yeah. Well I'm interested in this other guy. The one you asked us to look into. One Gary Drexel. Got an address on Alcala Park. But I've got a feeling that may be old. The license is due to renew this year. Good chance he's moved since this one was issued. Seems like everybody moves these days. You'd tell me if he was your client, right?"

"Probably not."

"But, since I'm a friend doing a favor for you…"

"He's definitely not my client."

"Then who the hell is? Look, man, this Fuentez guy is the third body that has some sort of connection to you. Even if it's tangential."

"Told you. Don't know Fuentez. Never heard of him."

"Well obviously, he knew Drexel. Had the guy's wallet. You remember Drexel," Ramirez said snidely, "the guy you're apparently looking for."

"Maybe Fuentez knew him, maybe he didn't. Maybe he picked his pocket, or mugged him. Who knows? Why don't you check with the Tijuana police, or their morgue?"

"Why don't you kiss my ass! I don't work for you, Ellis. You're stretching our relationship to the limit."

"I thought that's what friends were for," the P. I. quipped.

"Look," Ramirez said, "the whole point of this call was to let you know that your guy ain't residing in the San Diego morgue. But rest assured he's now on *our find-list,* as well as yours."

"Tell you what," Ellis offered, "whoever finds him first, lets the other guy know. What do you say?"

"I say, the next time we're face to face, you need to tell me a lot more than you're telling me."

Ellis began a series of phony sound effects, duplicating static as best he could, while knowing Ramirez wasn't buying it. "Ah… kishhh… you're breaking up, man… kishhh… must be losing my signal… .kishhh… we'll talk later." Just previous to ending the call, Ellis heard Ramirez say, "Asshole!"

CHAPTER 12

WHILE HE HADN'T PLANNED ON a quick trip to Tijuana, Ellis wasn't one to put opportunity on hold. He drove back to his apartment so he could leave his car in the secure garage. Driving it across the border was a non-starter. Not just because it would be a prime target for insurance-scam damage or theft, but also because of the cash-filled duffel bag in the trunk. Once his car was parked and locked, he placed a call to a contact he had in Tijuana. It was standard operating procedure for private investigators in San Diego to have liaisons in the Mexican border city. No P. I. would get anything done there in any reasonable amount of time without one.

Ellis's man was Jesús Medina, a twenty-something native who had grown up in the worst parts of the city and bettered his station in life by running errands for various cartel members. Up to this point, he had avoided the violent end that came to most flunkies associated with Mexico's toughest gangsters, generally by being obsequious and pliably dependent rather than autonomous and potentially dangerous. While Jesús worked mostly for the cartels, he wasn't averse to supplementing his income with tasks here and there for *gringos*, which the Baja *bandidos* found acceptable as long as it was merely gathering information, making connections, or simply being a go-between. And that's what the P. I. had in mind.

Ellis called Jesús, gave him Gary Drexel's name, told him what had befallen Victor Fuentes who turned up with the American's wallet, and said he'd be in Tijuana in two hours with two hundred dollars if the Mexican had good information, and five hundred dollars if he could actually put him in touch with someone who would have access to Drexel's whereabouts. Ellis felt he could be more generous with renumeration than normal having McCullum's retainer in the bank, even though he was getting increasingly concerned about mixing the father and daughter's assignments as well as their fees. For his part, Jesús knew he could trust Ellis not to ask something of him that would threaten his position with his principal employers. Plus dollar signs, ringing in his ears like cash registers going off, was a bit of an incentive as well for the Mexican. So a meet was set.

Ellis took an Uber to the San Ysidro Port of Entry and after showing his Passport to a U.S. Customs official, walked across the border into Mexico. Strolling into Tijuana always generated caution in the P. I. As he passed the pharmacies advertising over-the-counter medicines that one had to have a prescription for in the U.S., he always saw a steady stream of American seniors going in and coming out of the shops. Ellis couldn't help but wonder if he'd be like them some day in the future—looking for respite from pain wherever one could find and afford it.

Day or night, there always seemed to be a gaggle of U.S. servicemen, usually in groups of three or four, sliding in and out of the bars and talking to sharply dressed dudes eager to direct them to where the prettiest girls were—even virgins the *chulos* would insist—laughably. More often than not, there would still be a panhandler around asking if you wanted your picture taken beside his little grey burrow painted white with black stripes to look like a zebra. And there always seemed to be young men of one sort or another with recreational drugs for purchase, especially marijuana or cocaine. Unfortunately, the rise of fentanyl poisoning didn't seem to be having any adverse effect on street-corner sales.

Ellis always met Medina in the same place, the El Gato Blanco Bar. Day or night, no matter what time he showed up, the place was always open. It was the equivalent of a twenty-four hour McDonalds in the States. Of course, at the El Gato Blanco, there were no fries and happy meals, only tequila and happy endings. Ellis spotted the Mexican at a table by the back wall. Medina was trying to be inconspicuous but failing. His flowered shirt was too red, his creased slacks too white, and his pointed-toes shoes too shiny. It also didn't help when he spied Ellis and half-stood waiving the P. I. over.

"*Hola*, Señor Ellis. *Cómo estás?*"

"*Bueno, gracias*, Jesús. But let's speak English, please. It's a lot easier for me and I know how familiar you are with my mother tongue."

"As you wish. Should we… get on with it… as you *norteamericanos* like to say?"

"Let's do. I'm on a schedule. What have you got?"

"Enough not only for the two hundred you promised, but the five hundred as well."

"I'll be the judge of that," Ellis quickly replied.

"The man who had Señor Drexel's wallet, this Victor Fuentez, when he was still alive, he worked for the Ochoa cartel."

"Drugs?"

"Drugs mostly. Also prostitution and transportation services."

"You mean human trafficking. Smuggling people into the U.S."

"You call it smuggling. We call it traveler's aid."

"Forget what it's called. How did Fuentez wind up with Drexel's wallet?"

"I am not sure *how* he procured it, but I know he should

not have had it in the first place."

"Why is that?"

"It got him killed. That is why. My sources tell me Fuentez stole it and took it across the border to use in San Diego."

"Stole it from Drexel?"

"*Sí.*"

"You said he took it across the border. Does that mean Drexel was here?"

"*Sí.* Not only *was* he here… he *is still* here. And I can take you to him."

"You can? Jesús, you're a wonder. Let's go."

Ellis was about to stand when the Mexican said, "First, there is the matter of my fee."

"Take me to where Ellis is and I'll give you the five hundred there."

"Second, there is the matter of Ochoa's fee."

"Ochoa's? Are you saying the cartel has him?"

"He is, shall we say, currently their guest."

"Wait a minute. This doesn't make sense," Ellis began. "If Fuentez, an Ochoa man, stole his wallet, and the gang followed him into the U.S. and killed him… why didn't they take the wallet back."

"I didn't say the Ochoas killed him."

"Then who did?"

"This is undetermined."

"Let's get back to Drexel. You said you could take me to him."

"For the right price."

"We already agreed upon a price."

"That was the price for taking you to someone who knew where he was… not for taking you to him."

Ellis felt he was being hustled, but for the moment, he was willing to play along.

"Okay. Another five hundred for you. That's a thousand dollars, Jesús. But only if you put me in front of Drexel."

"*Sí*. That is very kind of you. One thousand for me. But it will be five thousand for Ochoa."

"Five thousand? Just to see the guy. Where the hell did that figure come from?"

"From Ochoa himself. Where do you think I got such good information?"

"What's the deal here, Jesús? Is this some sort of kidnapping scam? Are they holding the guy for ransom and just giving me a peek as some sort of proof-of-life or something?"

"Truly, I cannot say. I am not given such knowledge. I can only tell you that when I started making inquiries, Ochoa himself suggested this course of action. He said if you really wanted to see him, you'd pay it. And if you didn't, well, you'd just go back to San Diego."

Ellis started running the mental calculations, both

mathematical and moral. He had the $25,000 that McCullum had given him, so he could more than afford the Ochoa fee. Even though C. Tyler hadn't given it to him to find the son-in-law, he figured he might as well dip into it for that. Alex would probably reimburse him. After all, she was the one who wanted Drexel found, and Ellis remembered the look in her eyes when he told her what his fee would be to find her husband. She had expected to pay much more. Now, she'd have the chance.

But money aside, what about the principle of the thing. Could Ellis, in good conscience, leave Drexel with the cartel if he had an opportunity to free him? Well, that was putting the horse much too far in front of the cart. The P.I. didn't know if he'd have any say in the matter, especially since he hadn't brought any weapons with him across the border. Money, morals, opportunities, options—they were all bumping up against one another in Ellis's brain. So he decided to do what he frequently did in dangerous situations that he had little or no control over. He'd simply wing it.

Ellis told Jesús he was good to go, so Medina led them out of the bar, down the street, past most of the tourist traps, hotels, and open air vendors. He guided the American through a couple of alleys and into a section of town that appeared to be residential. They emerged from backstreets into a square lined with apartment buildings whose windows were jerry-rigged with pulley clotheslines for laundry to dry in the sun. The faded patina of pants, shirts, underwear and more provided at least some color to the drab concrete grey of the buildings themselves. A tiny park formed the center of the square where children played as adults sat and watched. Of course they watched their cell phones more closely than they watched their children, but such seems the nature of the times, Ellis thought, regardless of the country.

In front of a five-story structure, Medina told Ellis to wait while he went in to make sure everything was in order. When he returned, he asked for his fee.

"I can give you yours, Jesús," he said while virtually emptying his wallet, "but Ochoa will have to accept a personal check. I'm not in the habit of carrying that much cash around with me."

"He will accept your check, Señor Ellis. But make sure it is good. If it isn't, there will be terrible trouble for you… and even worse trouble for me."

"It's good. I just made a big deposit yesterday."

"Excellent. But don't tell Ochoa that. He will immediately raise his fee."

"You're not going in with me?"

"I will wait for you in the park."

"Which room is it?"

"Go to room 401. Knock three times. There you will find

Ochoa. Once his fee has been settled, you will be guided to Drexel."

"All right. Listen, if it's going to take long, I'll call your cell phone. If I'm not back in an hour, then—"

"No need to finish, my friend. The truth is, if you do not come back in one hour, you will not be coming back."

CHAPTER 13

AFTER LEAVING THE MILITARY, ELLIS had kept himself in shape by running daily. He didn't enjoy it like some people did, but it paid off in several ways. Such as climbing four flights of stairs in a building without an elevator. Outside the door with 401 on it, he prepared himself both mentally and physically for what he might find on the other side. It wasn't that he didn't trust his contact, Medina. He had no reason not to. There was no financial incentive for the Mexican to set him up. But he didn't know exactly what those who pulled Medina's strings had in mind. That gave him pause. Having come this far however, there was nothing left to do but knock, which he did.

A thin crack appeared between the door and its frame. The space was quickly filled with a salt and pepper beard attached to a man's face. The eyes looked at the P. I. but the mouth didn't open. So Ellis broke the silence.

"I'm Ellis."

Somewhere deeper in the room, he heard a voice say,

"*Déjalo entrar.*"

The bearded man opened the door wide enough for Ellis to enter. As he stepped inside, he couldn't help but notice that while the fellow kept his left hand on the door knob, his right cradled a forty-four magnum. It was in times like these that the P. I. had serious doubts about the career he had chosen.

"*Aquí atrás,*" came from the voice that Ellis had heard earlier. He knew that *back here* was less about providing information than issuing a command. So Ellis walked down the hallway with the bearded man and his gonzo pistol. They came to what appeared to be the living room, though it didn't look as if a lot of living went on in it. No paintings or photographs on the walls. No television set in the corner. No arm chair or reading light. Just one collapsible card table with three folding chairs, plus an upholstered divan. This was a transactional apartment, Ellis quickly decided, and today, he was part of the transaction.

Ochoa, or a man Ellis took to be Ochoa, sat on the couch smoking a cigar and depositing its ashes on the uncarpeted floor. He was a big man in a white suit, clean shaven, hair slick and combed straight back. His eyes were so brown they were black, and his countenance betrayed neither interest or boredom.

"Have a seat at the table," the man said in English.

Ellis walked over and sat down.

"You want to see the American?"

"Yes," Ellis responded. "Drexel. Gary Drexel."

"You do not have cash for the fee?"

"No. I don't. But I can give you a personal check."

"Make out the check. I'll fill in the name later."

"Alright," Ellis said, reaching inside his breast pocket, removing a pen and his checkbook, then starting to write.

"You realize that if this check were to bounce, so would your head... and that of Medina."

"I'm aware of the consequences. The check is good."

"Leave it on the table."

Ellis did as he was told.

"Edwardo will take you to the American."

"Should we need to speak again," Ellis began, "could I—"

Even more than the repetition, it was the tone of the man's voice that made it clear to Ellis he was being dismissed. "Edwardo will take you to the American."

The P.I. nodded and followed the bearded man out of the apartment and up the stairs to the top floor. There, Edwardo pointed with the gun still in his hand, saying, "*Final del pasillo.*"

The end of the hall had rooms on both sides. Ellis raised his palms and gestured with each as if to ask *which one?*

The gun barrel at the end of the bearded man's long arm swung to the right.

"Thank you, Edwardo, you've been very helpful."

There was no apparent realization of Ellis's mocking tone. Nor was there the courtesy of a reply as the bearded man simply turned and headed back down the stairs.

Ellis walked to the end of the hall and stood in front of the door on the right. He could hear music in the room. It was faint, but he recognized the song if not the singer. The Latin standard, "Besame Mucho," was wafting under the door along with the telltale smell of marijuana. He put his hand on the knob to see if the door was locked. It wasn't. Turning the knob as gingerly as possible, he silently opened the door and stepped inside. For a moment, he wished he hadn't.

Before him was a scene that instantaneously struck him as sad. Two people were dancing. Late afternoon sun spilled through the window and backlit their embrace while the sound from the radio filled the room with lyrics entreating *"kiss me, as if for the last time."* The pair swayed, barely moving. One, Ellis supposed, high on grass and the moment. The other in a seeming trance. No emotion of any kind on a face long absent from anything other than survival.

The man was Drexel. Even with matted hair, bags under his eyes, and a wardrobe that looked stolen from the wash bin at a homeless shelter, Ellis recognized him from his picture. The woman couldn't have been a day under seventy-five. She was completely naked and thin as a concentration camp survivor. White, stringy hair spilled down to her shoulders, while dark blood bruises spotted lined skin barely stretching across sharp bones. The nails on her reedy fingers were broken. The soot-covered heels and balls of her feet stepped not lightly on the floor, but instead, rested atop Drexel's boots, enabling the two to move as one. It was a scene out of some macabre fantasy. Unfortunately it was real.

Ellis spotted where the music was coming from. A radio on the floor was plugged into a wall socket. He walked over and pulled the plug. The love song ended and so did the moment. Without speaking, the old woman parted from her dance partner and walked to where a tattered dress was hanging across the back of a chair. She picked it up, not bothering to put it on, crossed to the door and left the room without addressing either man.

"Spoiled sport," Drexel said, moving to a small table and slowly sitting down in one of the two chairs that bookended it.

"Are you a hostage here?" Ellis asked.

"Only… in a manner of speaking," the stoned American slowly replied.

"Are they holding you for ransom?"

"I believe there was some mention of that."

"You've been having more than grass, right?"

"They seem to have… an inexhaustible variety of pharmaceuticals."

"Look, your wife is concerned about you. Why did you take off without saying anything?"

Pausing to collect his thoughts, which was difficult due to the amount of drugs consumed, Drexel replied, "Alex and I… had said more than enough to each other already."

"What about your son?"

"What about him?"

"Don't you think he'll be missing his dad?"

"No. I don't."

"Why not?"

"It's a long, sad story."

"Give me the abridged version."

The fog momentarily lifted in Drexel's drug-addled brain. "Who the hell are you, anyway?"

"I'm a guy your wife's paying to find you."

"Well, I guess you've just earned your money, then."

"Don't you want to get out of here? Don't you want to get back to your family?"

"I hardly think I'd be welcomed there."

"Why's that?"

"Well, you see… now you won't tell anyone, right?"

Ellis answered more expediently than truthfully. "Of course not."

"Upon my leaving, I took a little something to subsidize my declining years."

"What'd you take?"

Drexel, high as a windblown weather balloon, was incapable of discretion. "One of the old man's little horses."

"I understand he was collecting those for your son."

"My son, my ass. That bastard doesn't do anything for anyone other than C. Tyler McCullum."

"Do the Ochoa people know you took the horse?"

"Who?"

"The people who are keeping you here?"

"Of course not. You think I'd tell them? I wouldn't tell anyone about it."

"No. Of course, you wouldn't," Ellis said, as much to himself as to Drexel. "Where is it now? Do you have it here someplace?"

"Nope. Put it away for safe keeping. Before I ran into my current companions."

"Tell me about that. Tell me what you did?"

"Well, you see it's like this." As Drexel began to talk, he rose and began to pace back and forth between the table and the only window in the room. The window that was now sharing the last light of a vanishing day. "Having made some initial inquiries into the potential financial compensation such an item might bring, I was delighted to learn it was particularly substantial. So I decided to celebrate a bit and took the bus to Tijuana. But I was cautious, you know, not wanting to lose the thing, or perhaps become a victim of the rabid crime wave that seems to be everywhere these days. Not just here in Mexico. But in the states too. No city is immune, you know. It's bad every—"

"So," Ellis interrupted, "what did you do with it?"

"I was very cagey. I wrapped it in a silk scarf given to me by my wife, and put it in a bus station locker on the U.S. side of the border. Pretty crafty, huh?"

"Ingenious," Ellis replied, tongue planted firmly in cheek.

"Once here, I ran across some interesting fellows in a bar who kept the drinks coming and who supposedly knew some remarkably nubile adolescents looking for a good time. We left... connected with the youngsters... and partied for quite a while. I have to admit there was more than liquor involved."

"You don't say."

"I do say."

"And how did these people learn that you might make a good kidnapping prospect?"

"I was perhaps more talkative than I should have been. Probably mentioned I was a relative of C. Tyler McCullum... by marriage only, of course... but I'm not sure they comprehended that distinction. Everyone's heard of McCullum, you know. Even in Mexico."

"Let's get back to the miniature horse you put in the bus station locker. What did you do with the key?"

"Nothing."

"What do you mean, nothing?"

"Well, I just stuck it in the pocket of my jeans."

"They didn't search you? I mean one of them took your wallet, right?"

"Took my wallet from my back pocket. Took my cell phone. Guess they assumed I only had change in these pockets," Drexel said, slapping the front of both legs.

"You mean you still have it with you?"

"Yep," Drexel said, as he crammed his hand into the left front pocket of his blue jeans, pulled out a key with a number on the fob, and held it up for Ellis to see. "Got it right—"

Splink!

The window didn't shatter, it just formed hairline cracks around the small hole the bullet created on its way to Gary Drexel's skull. He hit the floor with a resounding thud. There was no doubt in Ellis's mind that the man he had just been looking at and listening to literally moments ago, was now irreversibly dead.

CHAPTER 14

DIFFERENT PEOPLE REACT TO SHOCKING situations differently. Most individuals who had just seen a man killed right in front of them would have immediately scrambled for cover and probably lost their lunch. Ellis, being ex Special Forces, had unfortunately witnessed similar scenes more than once. His response was more tactical than emotional. He bolted away from the window so as not to become a second target. Then he quickly rewound what he had just seen. Particularly the vision of Drexel's brain matter rocketing from his head and splattering on the floor. Since the displacement went downward, Ellis quickly surmised that the shot had come from a higher floor in one of the apartments across the way, rather than up from the street. And since there had been little sound—only the tinkling of the broken glass and no reverberating crack from the discharge—the P. I. assumed a silencer was used.

Both observations led him to believe that a well-trained marksman had made the shot, and that the prudent thing to do was to stay away from the shooter's sight line and get the hell out of there.

Prior to his departure, however, he was determined to secure the key that had been in Drexel's hand and now was only a few feet away, but directly in view of whomever had punched the ex-academic's ticket to extinction. What to do? From somewhere deep in the inner recesses of his hippocampus, he recalled an ex combat instructor extolling the virtue of making do with whatever was at hand. He quickly formed a plan and began to execute it immediately.

Unbuckling his belt and sliding it swiftly from his waist, he gauged the length required. Then he made a loop in one end. Balancing the capture and retrieval device in his hands, he tossed it forward much as if he were dealing cards. Bingo. The loop fell in just the right place to surround the key, enabling him to pull it over. Grabbing it, he quickly put the key in his pocket and his belt back on. Then he realized he was sitting on the floor next to something else that would help. While he hated to assail the dead, he felt that Drexel would understand. Well, being deceased, he wouldn't understand of course, but Ellis knew he certainly wouldn't mind. So he rose on his haunches, picked up the radio and tossed it directly at Drexel's body. The plastic and metal transistor bounced off the floor and banged directly into the very recent corpse.

Splink! Splink!

Two shots followed in rapid succession. One tearing into the radio, the other adding an additional hole in Drexel. But the diversion worked. When the flying music maker went one way, Ellis, flat on his stomach, scrambled like a lizard on steroids in the other direction. He was past the window, out the door, and on his way down the stairs before the shooter stopped cursing.

~ ~ ~ ~ ~

On his way back to San Diego, Ellis couldn't stop doing mental calisthenics. Once outside the apartment building, he hadn't stopped to look for Medina. He didn't think Jesús had anything to do with what had just happened. There was nothing in it for him. Neither was there any apparent angle for Ochoa or his henchmen. Why kill a potential money maker? Of course, kidnappers try to get ransom for individuals they've already murdered all the time, but if that were the case, a much more close up and personal method of dispatch would have been a lot easier. Alex had said she was afraid her father would do something rash if and when he located Drexel, but why have someone take him out before the stolen horse was recovered? And what about Detective Ramirez? Should Ellis call him? Let him know that the individual he was asking about was now deceased? That would surely lead to more queries. *How do you know? What do you mean you were there? What the hell's really going on?* All questions Ellis didn't want to answer just yet. And chances were, Ramirez would find out soon anyway… unless of course, the killer or Ochoa removed the body. The puzzles were piling up faster than the pieces.

Half an hour later, Ellis walked through the bus station terminal on the American side of the border with the key fob in his hand. It had a number on it, eleven; same as the figure McCullum said he was close to recovering. Weird coincidence? Or fate sending out vibes that things were going to get even stranger than they already were? Though there was no reason for Ellis to assume the shooter, or anyone else for that matter, had followed him to the bus station—just as there was no reason to assume that Drexel had shared information about the locker with anyone other than himself—still, Ellis couldn't keep from making an extra effort to be sure he wasn't being watched. So after twice scanning the surroundings for eyes turned his way, he made the decision to press on.

Approaching the bank of lockers, Ellis took one more look around before inserting the key in number eleven and opening it. There he saw a red and black silk scarf that probably cost more than the suit he was wearing. He reached in and put his hand around the folded material.

There was definitely something small and hard inside. Ellis wasn't sure why, but he thought he should unfold the expensive fashion accessory before leaving the key and the locker. He did so keeping his hands inside and out of view from any passersby. The palomino was there, intact, feet forward as if landing a jump. Ellis quickly wrapped the scarf back around it and slipped it in the left breast pocket of his coat. He then closed the door on the locker with the key still in it, turned and walked away.

~ ~ ~ ~ ~

It was late by the time Ellis got back to his apartment, and it had been a very long day. He initially felt that he should inform Alex of her husband's demise as quickly as possible, but then he reconsidered. If she took it hard, he'd be keeping her from a night's sleep. One she might sorely need in the days ahead. A few hours wouldn't really make that much difference. At least that's how he rationalized sending a text instead of calling, and asking if she could come to his office in the morning. She texted back and said she'd be there at ten. He went to bed. But he didn't get to sleep for some time. Even though sudden death wasn't new to him, seeing a life violently snuffed out in front of his eyes was going to linger a while. It always did.

Morning came and Ellis took the usual route to his

office. He swung into the Starbucks drive-thru and picked up two Americanos, assuming Alex was on her way. He made one more stop at a package store and picked up a half-pint of scotch. He didn't know how she'd react to the news about Drexel, but if needed, he wanted to have something stronger than coffee on hand. While he had bourbon in the bottom drawer of his desk, that wasn't her spirit of choice. He was thoughtful that way.

Ellis had only been in his office a few minutes when Alex arrived. She was wearing a long black dress that clung to her curves like wet paint. It ran from the bottom of her chin to the tops of her ankles and covered everything but hid nothing. Her red hair bounced. Her green eyes sparkled. Her French nails dazzled as she pulled her black leather bag with the gold chain from her shoulder, put it down on Ellis's desk and took a seat in one of the two chairs in front of him. Crossing her legs and meeting his gaze, she said, "I know, I know. But when I leave here I have to attend the Doan Foundation's Charity Luncheon and I want to make those stuck-up, grand dames envious and their husbands' pace makers skip a beat."

"You just might short them out completely."

"A little jolt to the system never hurt anybody."

"Let's hope so," Ellis said, as he began to question the timing of what he had to tell her.

"You know," he said, "maybe we should get back together later today. After your luncheon."

"No. Have people to see, places to go, things to do. Let's do it now. What have you learned?"

"Would you like some coffee? It's still hot. I just picked it up?"

"No. What have you found out?"

"I also have something stronger, if—"

"Stop the hemming and hawing, Ellis. It doesn't suit you. I told you the other day Gary and I are virtually estranged anyway. So tell me."

"I'm afraid it's bad news."

"How bad?"

"As bad as it gets."

"Gary's dead?"

"Yes."

"What happened to him?"

"He was shot."

"How do you know?"

"I was there when it happened."

"Where was *there*?"

"Tijuana."

"Did he suffer?"

"No. It was immediate."

"Who did it?"

"I don't know."

"You said you were there."

"I was. But it's complicated."

"Was my father involved?"

"I have no idea."

"Where is… the body?"

"I don't know."

"Can you be a little more detailed. I assure you I have no intention of breaking down and weeping all over your rug."

"I don't have a rug."

"Oh… you don't, do you? Well, you know what I mean. So come on. You've told me the hard part. The least you can do is fill in the details."

Ellis began with what he learned from Detective Ramirez about Drexel's wallet on the dead man, Fuentez. Then he told her he had a contact—withholding the name—in Tijuana who was able to put him on to her husband's location. He also mentioned the fact that it cost him five thousand dollars. He didn't mention the five hundred dollars he had to pay Medina. He figured that was the cost of doing business. He also left out details regarding the old woman in Drexel's room or the pursuit of young women that caused him to get kidnapped by Ochoa's people in the first place. Why add insult to injury. Ellis also avoided mention of the palomino miniature. In his mind, that was still part of his business with her father, not her.

"Sounds like a rather sordid end," she said.

"Many are," he replied.

"Well, like I said. We hadn't been a real husband and wife for some time."

"Yes. You said that."

"Are the police involved?"

"Don't know. They may not get involved if there's no body to be found."

"And why wouldn't there be?"

"Ochoa and his people probably don't want dead U.S. citizens turning up in their drug houses."

"I know you said you don't know *who* killed him, but do you have any idea *why*?"

"No."

"Could it have been random… some nut just looking for someone to shoot?"

"Anything's possible, I guess. Mexico probably has just as many wackos as we do. What are you going to tell your boy?"

"Tanner? Thankfully he's young enough I won't have to explain anything to him yet. When I do, I will have had plenty of time to sanitize something appropriate."

There was a slight pause as Alex looked out the window. Then she said, "Am I to suppose this concludes our relationship?"

"You asked me to find your husband. I did."

"And I guess you want your fee now. Along with that additional five thousand dollars you mentioned."

"There's no rush. I'm not in the habit of badgering recent widows."

"And how are you at comforting them?"

"Pardon?"

The next few moments would tax Ellis's character as well as his composure.

"You probably won't believe this, but I'm actually attracted to you. Even had the bizarre notion that you might have some stirrings toward me. In fact, what I told you earlier was only one reason I put on this outfit and dolled myself up. The other was… and please don't laugh… I wondered if our get-together this morning might lead to… what's it called these days? Is it still called a quickie?"

"Uh," fumbling, he said, "you have me at a disadvantage," admitting to himself that he had similar feelings since the first time he met her, but not knowing exactly how to react to her surprising admission.

"Well, if I have the advantage, I might as well press my lead. I wasn't kidding about a theoretical assignation. Here, I'll show you."

Alex rose, opened her purse, and pulled out a black satin thong. "Figured it would be easier to have this out of the way until we finished. But since it would be unseemly to engage in such tawdry behavior after just being told of my husband's demise, I'll just slip it back on."

With that, she put her purse down, turned sideways, bent over and slipped the enticing garment over her high heels, then proceeded to pull both it and her dress up high enough to land the underwear in its designated location. Using her index finger to brush a strand of hair in place as she headed for the door, she asked, "Lost for words?"

He was.

CHAPTER 15

AFTER ALEX'S DEPARTURE, ELLIS CONTEMPLATED what he had just seen and heard from his sexy client, what he had experienced the day before in Mexico, and what he was scheduled to do that night at the meet with the art dealer brokering—and perhaps now benefiting more than ever—from the deal with the recently deceased Edward Broadhurst. Having made the decision to finish the coffee he had purchased earlier, along with more than a splash of Bourbon to top it off, he was in the process of trying to sort out his thoughts by committing them to paper with his beloved and oft-used Meisterstück Gold-Coated Montblanc Fountain Pen, when he was interrupted by the arrival of two Chinese Communists.

"Mr. Brig Ellis?"

"Yes," the P. I. answered without rising from his chair.

"I am Baihu Chen," the diminutive man said. Then gesturing toward the fellow behind him—the man twice his size—the man twice Ellis's size for that matter—he added, "This is my associate, Weidong Zhang."

Ellis took a close look at both of them. Each rather resplendent in their white suits, dark ties, and Panama hats. An old Charlie Chan aphorism raced across his brain and thankfully not out of his mouth as he asked, "Do I know you gentlemen? Did we have an appointment I somehow forgot?"

"No," Chen replied, "we simply took the liberty of coming in and hoping you would have the time to see us."

"Well," Ellis said, "I'm usually at lunch now and my dance card's pretty full at the moment… but since you're here, I guess I can spare a minute or two."

"Very kind of you," Chen responded. "We will not take up too much of your valuable time. May I sit?"

"Be my guest," Ellis responded, gesturing toward one of the two chairs in front of his desk.

As Chen sat down, he reached over and took one of Ellis's business cards from a holder on his desk, glanced at it briefly, and slipped it into his shirt pocket.

While Ellis watched Chen take a seat, he also noticed the hefty Zhang reaching behind him and turning the dead bolt lock on the office door. The P. I. quickly realized the *wiser* part of valor was to unobtrusively pull the top right-hand drawer in his desk slightly open, affording swifter access to the Glock 19 nestled there.

Chen continued. "We represent the People's Republic of China's Ministry of Public Safety."

"Oh," was as complex a reply as Ellis could come up with extemporaneously.

"Here is my card," Chen said, handing it across the desk to Ellis.

The P. I.'s wit now working somewhat harder, he looked at the card with the photo of Chen and the Chinese characters surrounding it as he said, "It's Greek to me."

"Very humorous," Chen responded without smiling. "It is Mandarin, and basically confirms what I have just told you."

"Guess I'll have to take your word for that, won't I?"

"Yes. I suppose you will. Since you have apparently not taken the time to learn our language as we have yours."

"Chalk it up to my lackadaisical nature," Ellis responded.

"I think it is due more to your imperial hubris toward anything not American," Chen snarked.

"Alright, " Ellis said, "now that we've both insulted each other's country… with a dumb remark on my part and a rude one on yours… exactly why are you here?"

Before responding, Chen ran his right forefinger across the bottom of his thin mustache. A nervous quirk, the P. I. assumed. *Wonder what he has to be nervous about?* Ellis found out when Chen answered his question with a question. "Do you know a man named Edward Broadhurst?"

Shit, Ellis said to himself. *Just when I thought things couldn't get any more convoluted.* He tried to answer without answering. "At the moment, the name escapes me. Why do you ask?"

"We need to find Mr. Broadhurst."

They don't know he's dead, Ellis realized. *Guess that means they didn't have anything to do with him getting that way.* "No, I meant why are you asking me if I know him?"

"Rumor has it you might be planning to conduct some business with him."

"Well, if that were true… and I'm not saying it is… but if it were true, why would I want to discuss it with you?"

"Because Mr. Broadhurst is an international thief and smuggler. And he may be trying to move contraband stolen from the People's Republic of China."

"And what sort of contraband would that be?"

"A very rare, very valuable, objet d'art."

"You don't say. What kind of art?"

"A child's toy. But not just any toy. A toy with great historical significance."

"I find it hard to believe," Ellis began, "that a mere toy could engender such a response from your government."

"It is possible," Chen explained, "that this one toy could lead to others similarly taken illegally over the years. Broadhurst may be attempting to connect with a collector. We would like to connect with both."

"Do you know who this collector might be?" Ellis asked warily.

"Not at this time. But if we can locate Broadhurst, we can convince him to reveal the collector."

"And how would you do that?"

"By explaining the severe penalties for stealing from the People's Republic. And by illuminating how such penalties might be reduced were he to provide information that would lead to recovery of the additional toys."

"I see," Ellis said. "But what I don't see is why you're asking me about this?"

Reaching into his breast pocket, Chen pulled out a bright red pack of cigarettes with Chunghwa writ large above a likeness of Tiananmen with its Huabiao Columns. He tapped one out and quickly lit it with a silver lighter. Taking a drag and exhaling, the faint aroma of plums wafted toward Ellis. The P. I. could tell Chen was enjoying himself. So he said, "This is a non-smoking building." Even though it wasn't.

"But it's a private office," Chen responded.

"A private office whose tenant would prefer that you not smoke," Ellis said, even though it didn't really bother him. Stopping obviously bothered Chen. That's why Ellis said it.

Frowning with his eyes only, Chen said, "As you wish." Then snubbed the cigarette out on the sole of his shoe and tossed the butt in the Rubbermaid trash can next to Ellis's desk. "Now, where were we?"

Ellis rewound, "I was saying that I don't see why you're

asking me about this Broadhurst fellow you're looking for."

"His... trail... as you Westerners like to say... led to San Diego. We were subsequently informed that you might be involved with him."

"Informed by whom?"

"That... we are not at liberty to say."

"Yes, well suppose I'm not at liberty to say whether I know this Broadhurst or not. Unless of course, there might be some reward involved."

"Actually," Chen said, "there is a reward for cooperating with us."

"And what would that be?"

Chen answered straight-faced. "You get to keep the fingers on each of your hands... which my associate, Mr. Zhang, will remove, without anesthetic, if you do not stop these circuitous deflections."

"Why do I get the feeling you guys aren't really with the Chinese government?"

"Zhang," Chen said.

The silent hulk moved toward Ellis's desk, but stopped abruptly when the P. I. reached in the top drawer, removed his Glock, and pointed it toward him.

"Now," Ellis said, "here's *your* reward. You get to keep breathing as you turn around, Mr. Zhang. And you, Mr. Chen, may get up now so you can both go out the same door you came in. Once you do that, I'm going to place a call to a good friend of mine in the San Diego Police Department and you fellows will have a lot more than me to worry about."

Chen rose slowly, then before turning to go, looked at the P.I. and said, "Do not delude yourself, Mr. Ellis. Neither my associate nor I are the least bit worried about *you*."

CHAPTER 16

NOW, ON TOP OF DREXEL'S death, Alex's weird come-on, and his impending meet with Graves, Ellis had even more mental minutia to mull. Irrespective of what he said to Chen, he had no intention of calling Detective Ramirez. At least not right away. That would definitely lead to even more questions he wasn't ready to answer. *Hell*, he thought, he had questions of his own piling up like rush hour traffic on Interstate 5. Who poisoned Broadhurst? Why did the faux desk clerk wind up dead in a dumpster? Who shot Drexel and why? Someone put the Chinese twosome on to him, but who, and why? When was he going to tell McCullum that he had the eleventh palomino, and were he to be successful, should he argue that his fee be increased for returning two horses rather than one? Then, there was perhaps the biggest question of all… how the hell was he going to keep all this from Detective Ramirez with the body count going up faster than a private penthouse elevator?

Ellis's lack of answers were as plentiful as his questions.

He wasn't sure who poisoned Broadhurst, though he assumed it was the bogus counter man. He didn't know who punched the imposter's ticket or Drexel's for that matter. In the former's situation, he assumed it was to eliminate a no-longer-necessary appendage. In the latter's, it might have been retribution for his thievery. *Might* being the key word. He had no idea who put the Chi Coms onto him. And he planned, if all went okay with Graves, to simply turn over the eleventh palomino to McCullum when he handed over the twelfth. Of course, if history was indeed prologue, the meeting with Graves was destined for complications as well. As for filling in Detective Ramirez's information potholes, well, there were just too many potential pitfalls to pave that road anytime soon. After reflecting on all of his questions and a woeful lack of answers, Ellis decided that his best course of action was a run in Balboa Park, a recuperative shower, and a steak by the sea at Benny's on Harbor Drive. Not to mention a tumbler or two of Woodford Reserve before his ten p.m. appointment. *Yep, follow the poet's advice,* he told himself, *do not go gentle into that good night.*

~ ~ ~ ~ ~

Ellis arrived for the ten p.m. meeting at Grave's Art five minutes late. He didn't want to appear overly eager. There was an open space just two shops down, so he parked on the street rather than pulling into the alley where he had been advised to enter. The P. I. didn't like the idea of having his Mercedes in the dark where it might be more vulnerable to derelicts with nothing to lose or delinquents with nothing to do. He walked down the alley and spotted a door with Grave's Art stenciled on it. The duffel bag full of cash would remain in his car until he was satisfied the purchase would result in the object he had come for. He knocked on the door. It didn't take long to open.

"I'm Brig Ellis," the P. I. said, as he stared into the bespectacled eyes of a short, thin man in a blue blazer, white turtleneck, and gray slacks. He was somewhere in his fifties, Ellis guessed, and appeared calm, but cautious.

"Come in, Mr. Ellis, I'm Dudley Graves," the man said as he pulled the door back far enough for Ellis to enter, then stuck his head outside and looked both ways down the alley before closing it behind them. "Follow me, please."

Graves led the way down a dark hall until they reached what appeared to be a sitting room just off the primary gallery. A single track light overhead provided the only illumination. He motioned for Ellis to sit at a Chesterfield loveseat while he moved to a matching chair opposite.

The two men looked at one another. Each waiting to see who would begin. Ellis's patience won the standoff.

"You don't seem to have anything with you," Graves

said. "I assumed you'd need a briefcase, perhaps more than one."

"I have what's necessary in my car," the P. I. responded. Then, probing to see what kind of response he'd get, added, "We're waiting for Broadhurst, I assume."

"Mr. Broadhurst won't be joining us tonight. He's instructed me to execute the transaction."

"Really? When I talked to him, I got the impression he wouldn't miss this little sit-down for anything."

"An unexpected turn of events. He's content to have me accept payment for the item."

Again, a longer than comfortable pause in the conversation, this time broken by Ellis. "I wonder if I might see the item itself."

Graves appeared hesitant. Ellis sought to placate any inherent uneasiness. "Look, Mr. Graves. Both of us are longstanding members of the community. Though my line of work is considerably different that yours, I can assure you that I have no desire to do anything more than to finish our business. Once it's concluded, I'll continue with my small enterprise here in San Diego just as I assume you will with your infinitely more lucrative one. I suspect that's why Mr. McCullum chose us. We're just a couple of small fish in a big pond without grandiose aspirations."

"That seems rather insightful for a private detective."

"The occupation gets a bad rap."

"All right," Grave's said, reaching into his breast pocket and pulling out a slim leather case that could be used to house two cigars, or in this instance, an object that had already cost multiple lives. "I think this is the item in question," the art dealer said, opening the case and revealing a miniature palomino rearing up on its back legs, front hooves reaching for the sky.

Crack!

The first gunshot exploded the track light, plunging the room into darkness.

Crack!

The second followed almost instantaneously, ripping through Grave's back and bursting his heart on its way out. The force of the shot propelled the art dealer forward. His crash was so violent that both the case and the miniature flew from his hand and skidded across the polished wood floor—a floor like the rest of the room, now bathed in black.

Ellis had catapulted himself over and behind the couch when the initial shot took out the light. As he pulled the Glock from his shoulder holster, he heard Graves's body hit the floor, but he had no idea where the man or the palomino landed. For the moment there was silence. No sound was coming from the man he just met, so the P. I. assumed checking on him might be as lethal as it was futile. As would clamoring about in the dark looking for the miniature. The shooter, or shooters, would likely blast away at whatever sound they heard. Which gave him an idea. If he could draw fire away from himself, a muzzle blast would identify the shooter's position. Of course, if and when Ellis fired, it would give his own position away as well. And if there was more than one shooter, Ellis might wind up joining Graves.

Prudence definitely dictated staying perfectly still. Not moving a muscle until the assassin made a sound. He, or they, would move first, Ellis thought. Aggressors attack. They're hardwired to do so. He could just wait them out. Bide his time until a mistake was made. He could simply hold his position. Indefinitely if he had to. His will was stronger. He had more resolve. He was a lean, mean, *waiting* machine. Until he wasn't. Until he told himself that he wasn't going to squat behind a couch waiting all night for some mug or mugs to put holes in him. The more he thought about it, the more he thought *fuck it! Patience sucks.*

Ellis reached in his pants pocket and curled his fist around the loose change residing there. Pulling his hand out slowly, he pivoted on the soles of his feet so he'd be facing what he remembered as the majority of the room. Then in one silent motion, he tossed the coins through the air and up against the wall at the opposite end of the couch. Before they had a chance to stop jingling…

Crack!

A shot punctured the wall above the floor where the money had just landed.

Ellis saw the muzzle flash and returned fire in its direction.

Crack!

Shoot and move. Shoot and move, the P. I.'s mind kept saying. But before he had a chance to—

Crack!

It felt like an anvil had been heaved against the side of his head.

There *was* a second shooter, and he had just taken Ellis out.

CHAPTER 17

GRAZED IS A WORD THAT is frequently misconstrued. To the uninitiated, it sounds incidental, unimportant, hardly worth mentioning. To one who has been grazed by a bullet, it hurts like a son-of-a-bitch, and can often cause unconsciousness, or that foggy state between blackout and cognizance. Ellis got the whole enchilada. He didn't know how long he had been out, but he knew he had been. The crease along the side of his skull stung and throbbed at the same time. Blood had caked in his hair and on his ear. When he tried to sit up, dizziness and nausea made their presence known, making him think twice about the wisdom of getting to his feet right away. Somehow though, the darkness didn't seem as dark as it seemed before. Apparently his eyes had found a way to adjust. They had no problem focusing on the body of Graves lying nearby. They even spotted the case that the art dealer had opened to reveal the twelfth palomino. But look as he might, scanning the entire floor of the sitting room, he could see no miniature horse.

The thought of lying there for the rest of the night crossed his mind, because movement of any kind made the pain worse. But he realized the last thing he wanted was for someone to arrive early in the morning and find him lying next to a dead body, gun in hand. So he painfully and awkwardly struggled to his feet. He doubted that whoever put him down was still around, but he couldn't be sure until he made his way out of the sitting room. He did so carefully, not wanting to turn on lights that might attract unwanted attention. A few steps from the room he had just left, he came across an empty office. No point in searching it, he reasoned. Whoever killed Graves surely took the palomino with them. He moved to the main gallery and found art on the walls but nothing on the floor that shouldn't be there.

Next came a bathroom, whose sink and running water beckoned. Ellis took a handkerchief from his pocket, wet it, and as gingerly as possible attempted to wipe the blood from his ear and hair. He winced as he touched the crease that a bullet had ripped along his temple. At some point in time, a few stitches might be necessary. And it played hell with what was formerly a decent haircut. *Oh well*, he said to himself, *occupational hazard.*

Leaving by the same door he'd entered, Ellis stepped into the alley. Night air made him feel better—if only infinitesimally—but any relief was better than none. The space between the buildings was as unoccupied as it had been when he arrived, thankfully, and he turned to walk back to the street. A touch of dizziness came over him again and he stopped for a moment putting his arm against the wall of the building for support. He put his head down to see if it would reduce the vertigo. It didn't. In fact it caused him to drop to one knee and steady himself against the wall again. *Oh Christ, I'm going to be sick*, he thought, moving his feet out of the firing line of the rising bile in his throat. One, then another dry heave twisted his stomach.

His eyes watered. But suddenly, at least for the moment, nothing came gushing forward. He waited in his kneeling position, to make sure he wasn't going to leave the contents of his stomach in the deserted alley, when his eyes focused on something thin and white lying on the concrete. It was a cigarette butt, partially smoked. Not an odd thing to see in an alley. But something, some undefined notion in his aching brain, made him reach down and retrieve it. Standing back up with the cigarette butt nestled lightly between his thumb and forefinger, he looked it over, then brought it up to his nose and took a whiff. *Well, I'll be damned*, he said to himself, *plums*. Then, unable to quell the surging tide, the P. I. puked all over his loafers.

~ ~ ~ ~ ~

After taking a few minutes to recover, and using his blood-soaked handkerchief to wipe the splatter off his shoes, Ellis left the alley. The cigarette formerly in his hand had been dropped in the side pocket of his jacket. Walking toward his car, he did his best to determine what his next steps should be. Not an easy task when a bullet has recently carved a new part in his hair. Approaching the inanimate object he cared most about in the world, he cerebrally patted himself on the back for not taking the money with him when he went in the gallery. He was about to open the door of his classic Mercedes when compulsion forced him to make one last check before leaving.

Walking to the rear of the auto, he reached down to open the trunk when he noticed a scratch in the paint near the keyhole. A scratch? He hadn't scratched his car. He'd never scratch his car. If he did it accidentally, he would have used touch-up on it right away. He wouldn't leave a scratch on his baby. But there it was. A scratch. *Jesus*, Ellis said to himself, *can this night get any worse?*

It could.

When Ellis inserted his key and opened the trunk, the duffel bag packed with five million dollars was gone. In its place however, was a makeshift IED. The improvised explosive device was attached to a trip wire. A wire that Ellis had just tripped. The P. I. immediately threw himself backward and hit the pavement like a man trying to keep himself from being blow up. He was lucky. The car wasn't. The explosion lifted it off the ground and in the air, catapulting the body of the vehicle forward as the trunk lid, doors, windshield and more, flew out of the fireball and into the air. Damaged debris landed virtually everywhere in a thirty yard circumference. Incredibly, nothing heavier than a side mirror and tail light had fallen on the shaken shamus. But while his body wasn't broken, his heart was. Sure, he had failed to secure the palomino, but at least he now had an idea where to look for it. Yes, the five million dollars was missing, but lost money can sometimes be found. What really hurt… what cut deepest… the real dagger to his heart… was the 230 SL coupe. Some degenerate bastard had blown his ride to hell and gone. Now, it was personal.

CHAPTER 18

A TAXI DRIVER WITH CURLY black hair and a goatee to match, spotted a man on the street using a lamp post more for support than illumination. He pulled up beside him, put his window down and said, "Looks like you need a ride, dude."

Ellis wasn't sure whether he'd been standing there for minutes or hours. He was sure that he hadn't called for a ride, but he was more than willing to take advantage of anything that appeared to be good luck instead of bad. "As a matter of fact—"

Not realizing the P. I. was wounded, and just assuming he was drunk, the driver quickly began to rethink his position, "Not going to throw up in my car, are you?"

"Nope." Ellis replied. "Did that already. Don't like to repeat myself."

"Okay, hop in, then. Where we headed?"

Ellis opened the door, got in the backseat, and was about to give the driver his home address when his cell phone rang.

"Hello."

"Ellis?"

"Who else would be answering his phone?"

"This is Ramirez."

"Detective. What a surprise. Hearing from you at…" Ellis looked at the time displayed on his phone. It was past midnight. "Such a late hour."

"We need to talk."

"Funny. Thought that's what we were doing."

"Can the routine, Ellis, you need to come downtown, now."

"Much as I'd love to see you, Detective, I've got a rather splitting headache. Can't this wait until morning?"

"Technically, it is morning. And no, it can't wait."

"I take it this is a request, rather than a command."

"Take it any way you damn well please, but get down to the station now."

"Am I not at least owed the courtesy of hearing what this is about?"

"Well," Ramirez began, "I could tell you it's about your car that's in about a hundred pieces, which happen to be all over the street, sidewalk, and multiple buildings in close proximity."

"How do you know it's my car?"

"The license plate was embedded in a bus stop bench. We looked up the registration. Not all police work is nuclear physics, you know."

"Someone must have stolen it while I was asleep."

"You trying to tell me you were no place close to Grave's art gallery this evening."

"Do I strike you as an art lover, Detective?"

"No. And frankly, you never struck me as a murderer either, but there's a dead guy in that building which is just a few hundred feet from where your car blew up. And *his* opinion… when he had one… might be different."

"But what makes you think *I* was there. Maybe whoever stole my car just abandoned it."

"Abandoned it, and blew it up?"

"You know how destructive today's young hoodlums can be, Detective."

"And I suppose when we get the report back on the finger prints and DNA we recovered at the art gallery, yours won't be included."

"Well, now that you mention it, I may have wandered in there to look around before. I mean those particular sciences haven't achieved time-dating capabilities yet… have they?"

"There are also a number of bullet holes in the place. Some of the slugs we recovered. You telling me none of them are going to match if we do a striations test on your Glock?"

"How you'd know my gun is a Glock?"

"Paper trail, Ellis. Got records of every concealed carry swinging dick who purchases a weapon legally in the city, county, or state."

"Of course, the gun could have been in my car… which, as I said… could have been stolen."

"Ellis, that alibi has more holes in it than a hooker's underwear. And speaking of holes, there are a couple of Asian gentlemen who were brought in on slabs just a while ago with entry holes in the back of their skulls and exit wounds that took most of their teeth along for the ride."

The Chi Coms? Ellis asked himself, but what he asked Ramirez was, "Asians? Why would you think I had anything to do with Asians?"

"Because one of the two had your business card in his shirt pocket."

Ellis wasn't sure how, with his head still pounding like a toddler turned loose on a Chinese gong, but his brain managed to go into overdrive. "Ah, Detective… perhaps you're right. Perhaps I should come down. As it turns out, I'm not that far away. Yes. I'll be there momentarily."

Ramirez had no idea what caused the sudden turnaround. He was about to explore it when the line went dead.

"Driver," Ellis said. "Take me to police headquarters."

"Jeez. That's just a few blocks from here. You could walk and be there in a couple of minutes."

"Not in my condition."

CHAPTER 19

ELLIS TOLD THE DESK SERGEANT who he was there to see. The sergeant called Ramirez and got the okay for him to come up. When the P. I. walked into the detective's office, the cop stated the obvious.

"You look like shit."

"That's nothing compared to how I feel."

"Still want to try and convince me you were no place near a car bomb earlier?"

Ellis blew off his question and asked one of his own. "You know those Asians you mentioned, how long ago did your cleanup crew bring in their bodies?"

Ramirez looked at his watch. "Less than an hour, I think. Why?"

"Let's go down to the morgue so I can have a look at them?"

"What?"

"You want to know if I can identify them, right?"

"Yeah. I want to know that and a hell of a lot more."

"Okay. I'll fill you in. But after I've seen them, okay?

Let's go now."

"Jesus," Ramirez mumbled, getting up from his desk. "First you do everything you can to avoid cooperating, now you can't wait. What lit a fire in you?"

Ellis turned so his wound was visible. "The match that was struck on the side of my head."

"Damn. That's looks nasty."

"Probably appears worse than it is."

"Well, we're going to the right place to find out. Of course the sawbones down there aren't used to working on live bodies, but beggars can't be choosers, right?"

"Can we just go, already."

"Follow me."

All morgues are cold… and creepy, thought Ellis, including this one. At least they're not in the middle of an actual autopsy. *Thank the Lord for small favors*, he mused. But those weren't the only things on his mind as Detective Ramirez asked the coroner's assistant, "Can you show us the two Asians that were brought in a little while ago?"

The young man looked up from his paperwork and said, "Sure." He rose and walked toward a bank of individual vaults. Sliding the first one out, he read the name on the toe tag, "Weidong Zhang. Big fellow, isn't he? Looks like one of those Sumo wrestlers, huh?"

Ramirez corrected him, "Right size, wrong nationality."

Sumos are Japanese. Zhang is Chinese. Pull the other one out too, will you?"

The young man did as he was asked. "Baihu Chen," he said. "Yep. Chinese."

"Come take a look at these guys, Ellis," Ramirez said.

"I can see them pretty well from here," he countered, still halfway across the room.

"Come take a *good* look, I need to know if you know them."

Ellis started to take a step, then asked the young man, "What do you do with the clothes they're wearing when they're brought in?"

"We send them up to the evidence lab."

"Theirs gone up yet?" Ellis asked.

"Not yet. They're over in that bin," he said, pointing to a couple of open plastic containers on a countertop.

Ellis walked to the bin, rather than the vaults. He could quickly see that the clothes in one container were a lot larger than the clothes in the other. He drifted toward the smaller suit.

"Ellis, I already told you one of them had your card in his pocket. It's still there. The evidence techs will go over it."

The P. I. reached into the bin and fingered the suit jacket.

"Don't mess with that stuff," Ramirez said. "The lab boys will be all over my ass."

"Jesus!" Ellis shouted. "The big dude's getting up!"

Both Ramirez and the coroner's assistant jerked their heads back to the massive corpse. When they did, Ellis snatched the package of cigarettes from Chen's suit pocket and palmed it into his own.

Looking back at Ellis, Ramirez said, "Very funny."

The young man said, "We're not supposed to joke around in here."

"Made both of you look, though. Didn't I?" Ellis said with an infantile grin.

"Yeah, you're a laugh riot," Ramirez snapped. "Now get over here."

Ellis walked over and took a close look at each man.

"Well?" Ramirez said.

"As of now... I don't remember seeing them before."

"*As of now...* what the hell does that mean?"

"It means this injury to my head has me all screwed up, you know. It hurts. Everything's fuzzy. I'm nauseous. Thing's probably infected too. You don't want me to be sick again, do you?"

"Again?"

"It's a long story. And I don't even remember it now."

"Head injuries can be tricky," the young man said. "They can cause all sorts of problems."

"Can you take a look at it?" Ramirez asked.

"Sure," the attendant replied "Have a seat, here," he said to Ellis.

"Ah… you ever work on live bodies before?" Ellis asked.

"It's been a while. But I remember the basics. Let's get that wound cleaned. Looks like it might need a few stitches."

"A few?" Ellis exclaimed.

"I'll give you something for the pain. Might make you a little drowsy, though."

"Drowsy, huh? Well, go ahead then. But with the wound… and the stitches… and the painkiller and all… well, Walter, I just don't see how I'll be able to answer any of your questions tonight."

"He's right, Detective," the young man said. "Probably going to be pretty foggy when I'm through. Be good for him to get a full night's sleep."

"Great." Ramirez snarked. "Just friggin' great. Listen to me, Ellis, I'll expect to see you in my office by mid-afternoon tomorrow. And you will answer my questions without any of this *as-of-now*, crap. Do I make myself clear?"

"Crystal… as an opaque glass," Ellis answered.

The attendant was about to laugh, but looked at Ramirez and thought better of it.

Thirty minutes later, Ellis was standing outside the police station waiting for the Uber he had called. Detective Ramirez had declined, rather indelicately, Ellis's request to be driven home in a squad car. Payback for a decided lack of cooperation. So the P.I., now with six stitches in his head, stood on the corner waiting… hand in his pocket… fingering the red crush-proof box of Chunghwa cigarettes… the box with the twelfth palomino inside.

CHAPTER 20

THE DAY AFTER THE NIGHT before is always a bitch. Particularly if the side of your head looks like the Frankenstein monster and you can't stop mourning the loss of your car rather than the deaths of three men. The world is definitely up to its eyeballs in irony, Ellis ruminated, as he tried to take a shower without the spritzing needles pounding his recently sutured scalp. The stall was a little more cramped than usual this particular morning because Ellis's English bulldog, Osgood, had decided to join his master. This did, however, afford the P. I. the opportunity to share his thought process with his friend and confidant.

"So, I wind up with not one, but two of the precious art pieces I was sent to find, but I lose two rather important items... the five million dollars I signed for and my car. Since, in effect, he'll get what he was willing to buy, McCullum might or might not see the loss of the money as a risk of doing business with unsavory characters. Whether he does or whether he doesn't, I'm still out one fine automobile. My windfall case is blowing into a bit of a shit storm." Looking down at Osgood, he asked, "What do you think, boy? Is this one going to get worse before it gets better, or vise versa?"

The pooch didn't answer, but did attempt to lap up a lot of the water running down the drain. Soap appeared to be no deterrent.

After first drying himself off, then his dog, Ellis was one leg into a pair of boxer shorts when his phone rang. It took him another step and two more rings to get to it.

"This is Ellis."

"This is Alex."

"I know. I recognize *your* voice now."

"I have to see you."

"However… the *tone* of your voice sounds kind of frantic. Are you okay?"

"No. I'm not okay. I'm anything but okay."

"Hey. Take it easy, all right? Just tell me what's the matter."

"They're taking my son."

"Who's taking your son?"

"My father."

"You said *they*. You said *they're* taking your son. Who are the others?"

"I don't know. A man and a woman. I don't know them."

"Is the boy ill or something?"

"No. He's not ill. He's never ill. They just want to take him away from me."

"You mean… they don't have him yet? They haven't taken him away yet?"

"That's right. They don't have him now. In fact, they don't know where he is. I took him to a friend's house. He's safe there, unless they find him. Then they'll take him away. I don't know what to do. I only know I need help. Can you help me?"

"Listen, Alex, I'm not sure what I can do. I mean if this is a family matter, then me getting in the middle of it, well, I don't see what good that would do."

"Please. Just come talk to me. Help me think through this. Please."

The plea was plaintive enough to induce the desired response. "Okay. Just calm down, alright? I'll come see you. Are you at your home?"

"No. I'm at the Del."

"The Del Coronado? What are you doing there?"

"I had to get away. I had to take Tanner someplace safe."

"Wait a minute. I thought you said that you left your son at a friend's place."

"I did. But then I needed to be some place I could think. Figure out what to do. So I came here and got a room."

"Okay, what's the number?"

"It's 110. One of the beachfront cabanas. Please… come as quick as you can."

"I'll be there in less than an hour, all right?"

"Yes."

She hung up without saying another word. Ellis put down his phone and tried to put both her and the situation in perspective. Alex, a beautiful woman with more money than she knows what to do with, now has a fatherless son, and a father of her own apparently incapable or unwilling to consent to his grown child's wishes rather than interjecting *his* decisions and exercising *his* will. The dysfunction within the wealthy clan somehow made him recall one of his favorite novels, *The Great Gatsby*, and Fitzgerald's profundity: *Rich people only ever get richer, they don't get happier.*

Forty-five minutes later, a taxi let him off in front of the Hotel Del Coronado, a sweeping masterpiece of red and white Victorian architecture whose style was reminiscent of California when the state was still a golden dream. Familiar with the landmark, he strode through the lobby without asking directions and headed for the cabanas whose patios opened onto the Pacific. Finding number 110, he knocked on the door. No answer. He knocked again. Same response. Ellis gripped the doorknob, turning it slowly. The door opened. Loudly, he said, "Alex" before stepping in.

The room was like a watercolor, all sea greens and white, with just enough yellow to give a feeling of sunlight spilling here and there. "Alex," he called a second time, but again no response. Ellis moved past the king-size bed, turned the corner, and looked for the bathroom. He found it empty. Returning to the main room, he peered past the open French doors to the gentle waves caressing the sand that seemed to stretch as far as he could see in either direction. Then he spotted her coming out of the surf. Some strands of her hair were wet, but neither the sun or the Pacific were capable of dulling her mane's flaming red color. The green one-piece bathing suit clung to her as if it didn't want to let go. She strode toward the cabana looking like a sea nymph emerging from Botticelli's *Birth Of Venus*. The closer she came, the more the water droplets on her body made her freckles shimmer. When she walked across the patio and into the room, it took a moment for Ellis to compose himself. The best he could do was, "How was your swim?"

"God, that felt good," she responded. "I don't want that feeling to end."

Motioning to the towel she was holding in one hand, Ellis said, "Want me to help you dry off?"

"I just want you to help me," she said, tossing the towel to him.

He was about to reply when she began peeling off her swim suit. The straps left each shoulder simultaneously. Then she pulled them down farther until her breasts sprung from where they had been confined. They were each white as snow save for the freckles that ended halfway down and the pink nipples that stood erect from the cold water. She said nothing as she continued to pull the garment past her navel, over her other red hair, and then to the floor where she kicked it off to the side.

If she hadn't been so beautiful, Ellis might have been able to slow things down. If she hadn't been so bold, he might have debated more thoughtfully the consequences of his actions. If she hadn't been wet and tasted of salt water when she kissed him… he might have had a prayer.

"Ah," Ellis could only think to say, "do you need to take a shower?"

"Only if you want to take one with me."

"I took one before coming over."

"You're going to need another."

She was right. His clothes came off in stages. Fast and faster. He couldn't keep his hands off her and she made sure he didn't try. Their lovemaking bounced back and forth between the bed, the floor, and back to the bed again. There was no conversation. Words weren't needed. Ellis knew they would be later, but for the present he was unable to disengage from a coupling old as time, a wrestling both savage and sweet, a release exquisite as no other. In minutes, they were spent.

She slipped on a robe and he stepped into his trousers. They each took a glass of chardonnay from the bottle that had been opened before he arrived. Then they went to the patio and took seats facing the sea. There was no need to talk about what had transpired, its inevitability now obvious to both. Even ecstasy however, eventually drifts back to earth.

"Can you help get my son back," she asked.

"You told me he was with a friend."

"He is. I meant… can you help me keep my father from taking him away from me?"

"I'm sure a lawyer could help more than me."

"Lawyers are too spineless. They only want to play by the rules."

"Yes, but there *are rules* for this sort of thing. I suspect your father may already be taking advantage of them."

"But I'm Tanner's mother. Don't I have any rights?"

"Quite a few I would think. Haven't you looked into them yet?"

"No. I didn't think he'd actually go this far."

"Well, you are the boy's mother. I doubt he can do anything immediately about you having your son where you want him."

"Yes, but immediately doesn't last very long, does it?"

Ellis was hesitant to ask, but he did anyway. "He… your father… doesn't have anything he could use against you… with the court I mean… to imply you're not a fit mother."

"Certainly not. There's nothing like that. He just wants to have Tanner for himself."

Getting in the middle of family rows was about as inviting to Ellis as having a root canal. But he sensed Alex was really at loose ends and after what they had just shared, he felt compelled to help in some way.

"I'm about to conclude the work your father had me doing, so I'll talk to him once we've wrapped up our business. Maybe I can encourage him to give more consideration to what *you* want."

Ellis could tell that wasn't what she wanted to hear. She started to jerk about frenetically, quickly transitioning from her previously physically exhausted state to one of acute anxiety.

"But what if he won't listen. What if he doesn't care what you or I want. What if talking won't help at all. Can you do more? Can you make him change his mind? And if he won't, can you... somehow... just do what needs to be done?"

The construction was tortured, but the meaning was not. "Alex, I think you may have the wrong idea about me."

"No I don't. I don't have the wrong idea. I can tell by the way you made love to me. You want to do it again, don't you? You want to do it again and again. So do I. And we could you know. We could do whatever we wanted if my father wasn't around. Tanner could be our little boy. And think of all the money you'd have. You'd be richer than you ever thought you could be. You'd be fabulously wealthy, and we'd be a family, and I would make you feel incredible... night after night after night. Didn't I just prove that to you?"

"Alex," Ellis began, in as calming a way as he could, "the sex was wonderful. It really was. But it was just one of those spontaneous things that happens, right? I mean... surely it wasn't some tactic, right? Some ploy to get me to plot against your father?"

"Of course not. Of course it wasn't. I thought it was wonderful too. That's why I wanted you to think about being with me and Tanner. That's why I wanted you to at least consider it. You must have been thinking how wonderful it would be to have me every night, yes? You must have been thinking that. I could see it in your eyes. I could feel it when you took me."

Jesus, Ellis thought to himself, *what have I gotten into?* Maybe she's just upset. Overwrought because of what's happening to her and her son. Maybe that's what it is. Hopefully, that's what it is.

"Alex, like I said. I need to see your father. We'll wrap up our business and I'll talk to him about you and Tanner. That's a start, okay, But you should be getting with an attorney as well."

The light seemed to go out of her eyes. As quickly as she had gotten excited, she seemed to shift into lethargy.

Her body closed in on itself. She spoke without looking at Ellis. "Yes. I'll do that. I'll do what you say. But I'm so tired now. I need to rest. I need to lie down."

With that, she got up, left the patio, crawled into the king-size bed and pulled the covers up over her head. Ellis brilliantly concluded their conversation was over. Which at that moment, he saw as a good thing. The P. I. put on the rest of his clothes and started to say goodbye, then thought better of it and simply left.

CHAPTER 21

IF HIS MORNING HAD BEEN eventful, and indeed it had, Ellis wondered if his afternoon was going to be even more so. He was supposed to present himself in Detective Ramirez's office to answer a fusillade of questions regarding dead men, explosions, possible suspects, and heretofore unnamed clients that he still wasn't quite ready to name. The P. I. decided to postpone that meeting, preferring to avoid his friend on the force until he was at a point where he could actually answer the policeman's queries without one form or another of subterfuge. Ellis felt he wasn't far from doing that. So he switched his phone off to avoid what he knew would be Ramirez's calls, took a taxi to Ready Rent-a-Car, filled out the appropriate forms for a vanilla Japanese sedan, and headed toward the residence of C. Tyler McCullum.

Along the way, Ellis found himself exploring not just the havoc of the last few days, but also what might have induced it. He had been contracted to recover what was supposedly the final toy in a long lost set of toys that belonged to the last emperor of China. McCullum had mentioned there was a curse associated with the Twelve Palominos and maybe there was. Five recent bodies would seem to provide some support for that belief. Of course it was just as likely, perhaps even more so, that greed played a bigger role than spells in the rash of current deaths. At least that made it easier to postulate a motive for all the mayhem. And if the motive was greed, who might be the greediest? There seemed to be one option after another.

Broadhurst was a thief and smuggler who was ready to deliver the purloined palomino for a big payday. Whoever arranged to take him out, had to know of his plans from the get-go. The hostile poisoner, disguised as a hotel employee, served his purpose and was paid off with a bullet rather than a bankroll, obviously by someone tying up potential loose ends. Alex's husband, Drexler, was most likely whacked because he had the eleventh horse and someone knew it. Graves, the art dealer, knew that Broadhurst wasn't coming for the actual handover because he was dead. If Graves didn't have the balls to take two players off the board himself, he must have partnered with an individual who did. The Chi Coms either got wind of the buy, or simply followed an insufficiently cautious P.I. and planned to take both buyer and seller out while they snatched the horse for themselves. But someone put an end to them and their plans with extreme prejudice. It had to be someone aware that the deal was to be consummated at the art gallery and was perhaps serving as silent backup. Backup that didn't mind seeing Graves take one for the team and Ellis as the fall guy, if he happened to survive. It all seemed to be pointing in the same direction—the direction in which Ellis was headed.

At the gate barring entrance to the private road leading to McCullum's home, Ellis stopped, stared up at the camera, and waited to be recognized. It didn't take long. If sarcasm was liquid it would have oozed through the squawk box.

"Mr. Ellis, is it? New car?"

"It's a rental, Skeffington. Need to see McCullum."

"There's no record of an appointment."

"That's because I didn't make one. But he'll want to see me. I have something he wants."

"And what would that be?"

"As I said, something *he* wants."

There was an extremely pregnant pause before Ellis heard Skeffington say, "You may have noticed when you were here before that there is a grounds keeper's cabin about two-thirds of your way to the main residence. Mr. McCullum is there now. I'll inform him that you're on your way."

"Thanks, Skeffington. You're a prince," the P. I. intoned drolly.

The gate slowly opened and Ellis swung onto the private road. As he drove along the paved pathway, he ventured a guess as to why McCullum's man let him in *prior* to checking with his boss. Skeffington planned to intercept him. McCullum wouldn't be at the grounds keeper's place. Surely, if the lord of the manor needed to see his caretaker for some reason, he would summon him to the main house. It also occurred to Ellis that if the cabin was two-thirds of the route from the gate to the home, it was only one-third from the primary residence to the cabin. Which meant there was a very good chance he wouldn't be the first to arrive.

The P. I.'s mental machinations proved to be correct when he pulled up in front of the place. A white Range Rover was parked there. A man was standing on the far side of it. A man Ellis couldn't quite make out until he pulled right beside the SUV. Then the man stepped around the Rover looking like he had just walked off the set of *Downton Abbey*. He wore a Donegal cap, Galway boots, and a herringbone jacket. What really caught Ellis's eye however, was the Churchill 12 gauge double barrel shotgun nestled in his arms. *One of these days I'm going to learn to trust my instincts,* the P. I. said to himself.

For a moment, Ellis simply sat in the car with the engine idling and indecision written on his face. Skeffington read it and without raising his weapon said, "From this distance, if you attack I can blast the windshield into your face. If you run I can blow out your tires. Were I you, I'd simply turn the engine off and get out."

It seemed the better part of valor, at least for the moment, to do as he was told. Ellis cut the engine and stepped out of the car.

"McCullum's not here, is he?"

"How insightful."

"Walked right into your trap, didn't I?"

"Drove in actually, but why quibble."

"I assume all the security cameras have been turned off."

"For the time being."

"Is there, in fact, a grounds keeper?"

"Certainly. But he's nowhere around."

"How do you plan on explaining this?"

"Mistake, pure and simple. Caretaker took you for a vandal. Shot to scare you off. Unfortunately, his aim was bad."

"Unfortunate for me?"

"Precisely."

"What if he won't go along?"

"He knows where his bread is buttered."

"Our back and forth at the gate?"

"Easily erased."

"You cover your tracks pretty well, don't you?"

"A necessity in my former line of work. Brought to bear recently as well."

"Mind if I ask what that former work was?"

"Can't guess?"

"Oh… perhaps soldier… or is assassin a better word? What does the IRA prefer these days?"

"Very good. I thought I had extinguished all vestiges of my Irish accent."

"Doesn't pay to be overconfident."

"Is that what I am?"

"Not initially. You did things pretty well… up to now."

"Really. And just where did I go wrong? Enlighten me."

"You were in the perfect position to pull the whole thing off. McCullum shared with you what he was willing to pay to get the horses. You bet Graves was amenable to cutting out the middle man and keeping more of the take. So you and he hired a dude to pose as a hotel employee and poison Broadhurst. The hired hand's work done, you disposed of him. Understandable. The cost of a bullet being far less than whatever he was charging you. The night of the swap, you were there to make sure I'd deliver the money that you and Graves would eventually split. But there was a wild card… the Chi Coms. When the lights went out and the shooting started, they actually did you a favor. They iced Graves. Keeping you from having to do it later so you wouldn't have to share *any* of the proceeds. You had the advantage because they didn't know you were lurking about. So when they jimmied the trunk of my car and took the duffel bag with five mil inside, you followed, executed them, and took the money. Where was the twelfth palomino? You couldn't be sure. You may have searched them, but not as thoroughly as you should have. You didn't want to go back to the gallery and look… too dangerous. I might have regained consciousness. All that shooting might have been heard and cops could be on the way. To use a well-worn phrase, you took the money and ran. Back here of course. No point in having McCullum think you'd taken his dough. And you knew he'd assume I killed Graves and kept the money. Not to mention the palomino. That would probably anger him enough to ask you to eliminate me."

Ellis paused. Not just for effect, but also to take a breath after his Saturday matinée monologue.

"Sorry, must have missed something," Skeffington said. "Exactly where have I been overconfident," Skeffington asked.

"A couple of places," Ellis began. "When McCullum showed me the ten palominos he already had, and asked me to collect the twelfth, he mentioned there was no need to worry about the eleventh, because he already had that one secured. You two must have found out where Drexel was. You were to eliminate him, and get the horse back too. But it didn't work out that way, did it?"

"Were that the plan, I would have executed it flawlessly. But it didn't get that far. Additional information wasn't forthcoming. No further steps were taken."

"Are you telling me you didn't kill Drexel?"

"Why would I lie. I certainly don't need an alibi. I mean you're in no position to tell a living soul anything."

That doesn't seem right, Ellis quickly thought to himself. But he didn't have time to pursue the thought. He knew that time for talk had come to an end.

"And the other instance you believed me overconfident?"

"You let me out of the car," Ellis said. Then, with the speed and impact of an NFL linebacker, he barreled into the Irishman's knees. The force was such that it initially knocked Skeffington back against the Range Rover then ricocheted him forward as his feet were caught beneath Ellis. When he toppled over, still holding onto the shotgun, Ellis scrambled up and grabbed the weapon before it could be turned toward him. Now both men had hands on the 12 gauge and were struggling for control. Pulling. Pushing. Pushing. Pulling. It was a test of strength neither could afford to lose. While grappling over command of the weapon, they managed to struggle to their feet. Still locked in an intense battle for possession, neither would loosen their grip. The two were face to face, each holding on literally for dear life. Like muscle memory reverting to rote instruction, Ellis's hand-to-hand combat training kicked in. He cocked his neck back, then snapped it forward, head-butting Skeffington across the bridge of his nose. The Irishman's beak split like a cracked egg, and red blood, not yellow yoke, spilled down his face and began to run into his mouth. The blow however, loosed his grip not one bit. As Skeffington grinned through crimson teeth, Ellis immediately recalled what McCullum had told him about the Irishman. *He suffers from CIPA… congenital insensitivity to pain… you could cut out his kidney without anesthetic and he wouldn't feel a thing.* Which certainly wasn't the case with Ellis. His involuntary headbutt reverberated through his own skull like a bowling ball busting a ten pin strike, especially along his bullet-wounded scalp that had just been stitched up the night before. Timing of the pain was delayed but not the least bit retarded in intensity. An electric jolt ran along the suture line. Ellis felt like the side of his head was being pried apart with a can opener. But still he maintained his white knuckle grip on the weapon.

There is a moment in any test of strength, when one man knows the other is going to win. That moment came for Ellis when his fingers began to tingle and ache and to ever so slightly give way. He knew instinctively that if tried to hold on longer, or possibly re-grip, he'd lose control. Only two options sprung to mind. He could knee Skeffington in the balls... but the bastard wouldn't even feel it... so his alternatives were down to one. Ellis moved his right leg out to the side then swung it back with all the force he could muster to knock the Irishman off his feet. When his leg crashed into his opponent's, he also pulled as hard as he could throwing himself backward to flip Skeffington over him and jerk the gun away. The pair catapulted over one another like bounding tumbleweeds. The maneuver had worked. They were now separated. But Skeffington was the one holding the shotgun. And Ellis was looking down the barrel.

"Wait!" Ellis yelled.

"For what," Skeffington responded, "your services, Mr. Ellis, are no longer needed."

"But... you can't shoot me."

"Oh really. Why is that?"

"Because I have the last two palominos with me," Ellis said, patting the left side of his coat. "If you shoot, you'll destroy them."

"If I shoot center mass, I might," Skeffington quipped. "But if I simply blow your head off, it won't really matter, will it?"

Before Ellis could answer, the roar of a car made both men's heads snap to the side as it streaked like a screaming Mimi down the private road toward the main house. It was less than a second's diversion, but it was the millisecond the P. I. needed. As each man turned to look back at one another, Ellis had already pulled the Glock from his shoulder holster and swung it up in time to get off a shot. The bullet went into Skeffington's right eye, through his brain, and out the back of his skull. It didn't hurt him, but it killed him instantly.

CHAPTER 22

WHEN ELLIS ARRIVED AT THE main house, there was a car in the driveway. *That's the car that flew by when Skeffington and I were previously engaged*, the P. I. realized. *I owe the driver a big thank you.* But then he thought first things first as he bounded up the steps, tried turning the knob on the front door, and surprisingly found it unlocked. Opening the door, he entered cautiously. He had just gotten out of one scrape. He wasn't in a hurry to get in another.

The P. I. stepped slowly down the main hall that centered the house. As he walked, he could see into open rooms on either side of him. They were all empty until he reached the study where McCullum had taken him before. There he found the master of the house at his desk. Sun streaming through the floor-to-ceiling leaded glass window threw rays across McCullum's form slumped over papers he had apparently been perusing. His hat was still atop his head and a pen stood vigil between the fingers of his hand. He was either dead or asleep. Ellis couldn't tell which. Until

McCullum twitched, jerked twice, then moved his chest off the desk and pushed back into the tall chair in which he sat. That's when he noticed the P. I.

"No one was at the door, so I let myself in," Ellis said.

"Caught me catnapping, did you? Oh, well. One of the indignities of old age. There are quite a lot of them. You look a bit the worse for wear yourself, Mr. Ellis. Have an automobile accident on the way over or something?"

"More in the *or something* category."

"I can have Skeffington get you something to clean up with if you like?"

"Actually, you can't."

"I can't. Why is that?"

"Because Skeffington is dead."

"Dead? What in the world are you talking about?"

"I look the way I look because your man, Skeffington, tried to kill me. Trust me. He now looks a lot worse than I do."

McCullum seemed genuinely confused. "Why would Skeffington want to kill you?"

"To keep you from finding out what he'd been up to. Skeffington was in league with Graves. They had Broadhurst killed so they wouldn't have to split your five million with him. Oh yeah, Graves is dead too."

"Graves, dead. Did Skeffington do that?"

"No. A couple of Chinese types. They were after the palomino as well. If they hadn't killed Graves, I'm betting

Skeffington would have. He wasn't exactly into sharing."

"I find all this hard to believe. Skeffington seemed such a loyal man."

"Loyal to himself. Five million dollars will do that. Plus a chance to get the twelfth palomino for himself and sell it again."

"Where is that five million by the way? As memory serves, I believed you signed for it."

"Yeah, I signed for it. But the Chinese took it away from me when they gave me this," Ellis said, pointing to his head wound. "Then Skeffington took it from them before he turned out their lights. Chances are, he probably hid it in his room or around here somewhere. He didn't have time to bank it."

"Oh well," McCullum fluffed, "I'm sure we can locate it. It's of no consequence anyway."

"No consequence? Five million bucks! It cost six men their lives."

"Six criminals… or would-be criminals according to you. And the money's not that important because it's counterfeit."

"Counterfeit? You gave me bogus money to make a dangerous deal with?"

"When one is in a game with thieves and scoundrels, it is sometimes necessary to revise the rules. But let's get to the heart of the matter. Where is the twelfth palomino?"

Ellis reached into his coat pocket and pulled out the miniature horse. The one with its front hooves reaching skyward. He stepped forward, leaned down, and placed it on the desk in front of McCullum.

"Beautiful. Just beautiful. The Twelve Palominos… at last."

"Well," Ellis commented, "it's only the twelfth if you have the eleventh."

"I believe I told you that was being taken care of."

"You did. But I'm not sure it was taken care of in the manner you thought it would be. Here it is," the P. I. said, reaching in his other pocket and pulling out the palomino landing a jump. He set it beside the other on the desk.

McCullum looked at the two horses. Then he raised his head and looked at Ellis. "And just how did *you* happen to come upon the eleventh?"

"Apparently, I was in the right place at the wrong time. Had to take it off a dead man we haven't mentioned yet. Your son-in-law."

"Drexel, dead?" McCullum's surprise seemed real, but short-lived. "I can't really say I'm sorry, but it didn't have to end that way. Did Ochoa's bunch kill him? And how did *you* get involved?"

"There are more important questions to me, " Ellis came back quickly. "Like how do you know about Ochoa's involvement? And when did you dispatch Skeffington to kill Drexel and retrieve the horse?"

McCullum gave Ellis a look to make sure the P.I. knew he was annoyed at the accusation. Then he went into an explanation. "I was contacted by one of Ochoa's surrogates who let me know they had my daughter's husband. He said he'd get back to me with a ransom demand and instructions on how to deliver it. Frankly, I assumed Drexel was colluding with Ochoa. Probably came up with the scheme himself to bilk even more dollars out of me. But I never sent Skeffington, because I never got all the details. They were supposed to come in two phone calls. The first, giving me a location in Tijuana. The second, would be the amount of money and how they wanted it broken up. I got the first call, but haven't had a second. And I never sent Skeffington anywhere."

Ellis wasn't surprised that McCullum was denying involvement in Drexel's death, but Skeffington denied it too. Maybe they weren't involved. But if not, who did kill Drexel?

"Did anyone else in the household know about the situation with your son-in-law?"

"No," McCullum answered, "I'm not in the habit of sharing family problems with the help."

The word *family* struck a chord. A chord for a concerto he wasn't sure he wanted to hear. So he started circuitously. "There's a car parked out front. Do you know who it belongs to?"

"What kind?"

"BMW, I think."

"Color?"

"White."

"Belongs to Alex. She comes and goes out of here all the time like a whirling dervish. Seldom remembers to lock the door."

"Is there any way Alex might have known about Drexel's situation?"

"Anything's possible, I guess. Drexel might have contacted her himself. Or she might have listened in on my phone conversation. She's been known to do that from time to time. How do I know? A breath taken in a pause. The sound of a phone being hung up before mine. I'm afraid she's not the most subtle eavesdropper ever. Still, she is my daughter and I do love her."

"Love her, do you?" Ellis's words sounded more critical than questioning. "Is that why you're trying to take her son away?"

"For Christ's sake… what are you talking about now."

"Alex told me you were going to take Tanner away from her. That you and others would be taking the boy right now if you could find him."

"Find him? I know exactly where he is. What makes you think I don't?"

"Alex told me she had to hide him at a friend's place… a place you're not aware of."

"Alex tells people many things, Mr. Ellis. Most have only a tangential connection to the truth."

McCullum's comment triggered a flashback in Ellis's mind—he and Alex finishing drinks at Benny's—Skeffington appearing, picking up the check and saying, *"I'd be wary of anything Ms. Alex has to say… she's an inveterate liar."* Where the hell was this going? Ellis had to know. He pressed.

"So just where is the little boy… Tanner… where is he now?"

McCullum rose from the chair behind his desk, picked up the eleventh and twelfth palominos, walked to the glass case holding the rest, opened it, and placed them in line with the others. As the old man looked at them wistfully, Ellis sensed he was debating *how* or *whether* to respond to the P. I.'s question.

"Have a seat, Mr. Ellis. That wound of yours looks like it might need some additional dressing. Reaching for the phone he said, "Should I ask the housekeeper to bring in some bandages?"

"It's okay for now. What about my question?"

McCullum put the phone down, saying, "You've been through quite a lot the last few days. All in service to me, I suppose. So I'm going to share some things with you. Things I'm not in the habit of sharing. Please, sit down."

CHAPTER 23

ELLIS TOOK A SEAT IN front of the desk. McCullum began to pace as he spoke. "The direct answer to your question is that Tanner is not with Alex's friend. Alex has no friends. Tanner is at The Hyperion Academy. It's an outrageously expensive boarding school for those wealthy enough to purchase the kind of support for their children that they're either unable or unwilling to provide in a home environment. Tanner is four years old now. Alex hasn't seen the boy in person for two years. Whatever she told you is either a fantasy or a lie. She experiences a number of the former and there seems to be no end to the latter."

Ellis didn't interject. He didn't know whether to challenge what McCullum was saying or not. But he knew he wanted to hear whatever the man had to say.

"You see my daughter suffers from an extreme bipolar condition. It's actually a form of schizophrenia. Her malady often results in social isolation and aberrant behavior, as well as delusions. Years of therapy and vast quantities of medication have shown some positive effects. Yet both are incapable of totally controlling, and certainly not eliminating, the disease itself. Alex's current separation from Tanner is the result of a court order. You see, Mr. Ellis, two years ago my daughter tried to kill her son. She was in the process of drowning him in the bathtub when our Philippine housemaid risked her own life to save the boy. Over the years Alex has variously blamed me, her recently departed husband, and occasionally UPS, Federal Express, and Amazon delivery men for keeping her separated from her child. Whatever she told you will likely not be remembered by her the next time you meet."

Ellis wasn't sure how to respond. The absence of pleas for compassion or understanding in no way diminished the pain apparent in McCullum's recitation. If anything, their nonexistence somehow made the sad account even more credible.

The P. I. began, "I suppose... in addition to treatment... you've thought about things that could have been done differently in the past. Something that might have... I don't know..."

"Everything could have been done differently, Mr. Ellis. I could have spent more time with her and her mother... who, took her own life, by the way. Don't get me started on that, please. I could have raised Alex more like a daughter and less like the son I wanted. I could have done virtually everything absolutely ass-backward to the way I did... and the doctors tell me it wouldn't have made one iota of difference to her mental condition. I'm not sure if they tell me that to actually assuage my regret, or to simply keep my checks coming."

"You said you raised her more like a boy. What did you mean?"

"Mostly in physical ways, I guess. I avoided the girlie, frilly things, and taught her how to sit a horse, catch a fish, shoot a gun. Figured she'd pick up the feminine attributes on her own... some way."

"You say you taught her how to shoot. What sort of weapon?"

"Rifles mostly. Took her to gun ranges. Hunting too. She proved to be quite the marksman. Or these days it would be marksperson, I guess."

Ellis heard the quip but he couldn't get past the sentence that proceeded it. Particularly with Skeffington and McCullum both denying involvement in Drexel's death. Skeffington had the drop on Ellis at the time. He had no need to lie. If Alex did overhear the designated location, and like McCullum said, also blamed her husband for her separation from Tanner... all of a sudden connecting the dots became unfortunate, but unavoidable.

"There's a real probability," Ellis began, "that Alex needs even more help than she's getting."

McCullum walked in front of the massive window, looked out, then turned and faced Ellis. "What exactly are you saying?"

"You said she tried to kill her child."

"That was two years ago. We've gotten Tanner out of harm's way. Plus, there have been no similar episodes with Alex since then."

"None that you know about."

"What do you mean?"

As Ellis began to share his thinking with McCullum, neither saw the silhouette top the hill that separated the stable from the house. Initially backlit by the setting sun, it formed the outline of a horse and rider in full gallop. At its present distance from the home, even if they had seen her, they wouldn't have been able to make out exactly who was in the saddle dressed in full riding gear. But the distance to the home was being shortened moment by moment.

Alex leaned forward and crouched low over the majestic palomino, Emperado. She used a riding crop and her boot heels to spur him on with all the speed he could muster. Horse and rider were one, sprinting hellbent toward the streaks of sunlight glancing off the windowpanes.

Ellis was completing his explanation of why he believed Alex killed Drexel, and was a threat to herself and others, when he looked past McCullum's shoulder and spotted the onrushing twosome.

"Jesus! Is that—"

McCullum saw the distress in Ellis's gaze. He quickly turned on his heel and looked out the window that towered before him. There was only time for him to utter, "Oh my God. No."

It sounded as if the world had split into pieces. Glass and leading thundered and shattered, sending slices rocketing throughout the room. Alex flew off the back of the horse like a daredevil being shot from a canon in a circus act. She slammed on the desk first, bounced off the top of it into the bookshelves, then careened to the floor. Emperado, already wild-eyed, went even more berserk. Blood was streaming from gashes in its forehead and muzzle. Shards of glass were impaled in its barrel and hindquarters. The stallion's eyes were darting madly as it reared up on its hind legs, hooves clawing at the air. The frightened horse was so overwrought it defecated profusely. When its front legs joined the back two on the floor, the once disciplined mount turned into a traumatized animal. It began jumping and staggering around uncontrollably; its massive head and neck knocking over everything in its path. Floor lamps toppled. The giant mahogany globe was knocked off its axis and rolled into the red leather chair that slid across the room like it was on ice. Ellis was on his feet and trying to get to Alex. McCullum had risen from the Chesterfied he had fallen onto when horse and rider came through the window. He was doing all that he could to approach Emperado and calm him down, but was having no success whatsoever.

Then fate, fear, or continuing frenzy accelerated the stallion's shock. He jerked his forelegs up and into the air again. This time they crashed down and smashed the redwood stand in the shape of a crown. The stand with the glass case that housed the twelve palominos. The miniatures burst from their splintering refuge like roaches roused by unexpected light. They wound up all over the floor. The floor directly beneath the still crazed fourteen hundred pound beast who recklessly stomped the miniature horses into broken pieces, one after another. Alabaster disintegrated into minuscule gravel. Emeralds imploded into green tinged sand. All were crushed and demolished irreparably. The fabled twelve palominos, recovered from clandestine locations around the world, had finally completed their epic journey from legend to oblivion.

CHAPTER 24

THE AFTERMATH OF CATASTROPHE CAN sometimes exceed the ordeal of the calamity itself. While humans have a capacity for survival, it is not always an existence that is welcomed. So it was with Alex. When she fell, she hit head first. The riding helmet she was wearing spared injury to her brain, but the impact broke her neck, shattering the first and second vertebrae. The thirty-two year old woman was paralyzed from the neck down. An operation to attach her spine back to her skull was deemed successful—if one deems spending the remainder of one's life in a wheelchair, attached to a ventilator, a success. She still knew who she was and what she had done, though she couldn't really come to any conclusion as to why she had done it. She had no memory of the child she bore or the husband she killed. The most expensive psychiatrists money could buy couldn't reach an agreement on the wisdom of filling in the blanks. A decision, made by her father, was to keep those facts from her until such time she asked about them herself, or her son, Tanner, was old enough to desire a relationship with his mother and to understand the impaired state of mind that led to her fate.

Emperado was put down. The noble steed's injuries, as well as his resulting mental condition, were considered beyond repair. To carry on his princely line, the horse's sperm was salvaged and cryopreserved, later to be used in subsequent breeding. The twelve palominos may have been lost forever, but the great stallion was destined to keep the breed going long after his untimely demise.

C. Tyler McCullum was medivacked from the back lawn of his home to the rooftop of Sharp Memorial Hospital in San Diego. There he was rushed to an operating room where surgeons replaced the blood he had lost from the broken leg he sustained when he finally reached Emperado to try and calm him and was kicked through the shattered window for his efforts. The surgeons were able to avoid amputation and the need for a prosthetic device by initiating advanced microscopic and robotic surgical techniques yet to be approved by the state of California or the FDA. Wealth has its privileges.

Ellis was unharmed save for a few cuts on his hands and the bullet wound in his scalp that reopened and had to be stitched again. Even with the additional tailoring, from that moment on he would have a permanent scar on the right side of his head which he would frequently refer to as his saber wound. He was, after all, a hopeless romantic.

The P. I. met with Detective Ramirez a day after the disaster. He consumed four cups of coffee over the course of two hours while answering questions and providing comprehensive information about who shot whom and why. Granted, many of his insights were gleaned through what lawyers might call hearsay, but Ramirez wasn't an attorney, and because of their longstanding relationship, believed that Ellis truly believed what he was saying. While the P. I. was thorough, he did decide to leave out the fact that the five million dollars was counterfeit money. No need to open that potential can of worms, Ellis thought, after everything that his client had been through.

Through their give and take, it appeared to both men that while the letter of the law had been undeniably mangled, justice had perhaps been served across the board. The killer of Broadhurst received his with a bullet. Graves' murderers, the Chi Coms, got their penance from Skeffington. Skeffington was served his sentence from Ellis. That left Drexel's death. And while the hapless former teacher had indeed been snuffed out with malice, it would be virtually impossible to say that his killer got off without retribution. The idea of seeking prison confinement for a mentally disturbed, paralyzed woman who couldn't even breathe on her own, was in neither the P. I.'s or the detective's code of conduct.

While there was some measure of agreement that all

of the mayhem that transpired was due to McCullum's attempt to traffic in stolen goods, there was complete concurrence that high-priced attorneys and high-level connections would never allow a case to even be brought against him. And, when one came right down to it, the two acknowledged that his atonement would be living out the years he had left with the realization that his covetousness had led to all the carnage.

Ellis's session with Ramirez ended with both men shaking hands and the P.I. agreeing to be a lot more cooperative a lot earlier in any future investigations. The two parted as the longtime friends they had always been. Ellis wasn't sure when they'd touch base again, but he knew they would. Just as he knew he'd be making one more visit to the home of C. Tyler McCullum.

CHAPTER 25

IN THE WEEKS THAT FOLLOWED the devastation, McCullum hired a temporary administrative service to oversee his appointments. Ellis called to make one. The P.I. requested that he be able to see Alex alone before meeting with her father. The temp in charge sought permission. It was granted.

Upon arrival, the housekeeper met Ellis at the door and led the way to an upstairs bedroom. Climbing to the second floor, he couldn't help but notice that an independent elevator had been added by the staircase. There was no doubt who that was for. The second floor corridor was shaped like a horseshoe, with multiple rooms rimming the curve. The housekeeper stopped at a door in the middle. She motioned to the latch and said, "Ms. Alex is expecting you." Then she turned and walked away.

Ellis slowly opened the door and stepped inside. Light filled the expansive space via windows that stretched from one side of the room to the other, creating a sweeping vista of green rolling hills with the snow white stable in the foreground. Drapes had been pulled back to each corner to highlight the view. However, Ellis couldn't help but wonder if the occupant really preferred it this way, or whether it had simply been done to keep visitors from feeling uncomfortably confined with the individual forever confined to more than just her room.

She was in a wheel chair facing out the window. Looking at the back of her head he could see that her once shoulder-length hair had been cut short and lay tight against her head like one of those twenties flappers he often saw portrayed in movies and pictured in magazines. Even at that length however, it was still the burning red color he remembered. That, and the feel of it lying across his chest.

"Hello, Alex," he said. "It's Brig. Brig Ellis."

She pushed a button on the arm of the chair. There was a slight whirring sound as it automatically turned itself around. When it did, he could see the breathing device attached with the tube connected to a collar around her neck. Ellis hoped his face gave no clue to the sorrow that had suddenly overtaken him.

"You think I wouldn't recognize your voice," she said, still with a bit of a mechanic drone. "Though I bet you wouldn't recognize mine now, would you?"

"I think I would," Ellis said honestly.

"Liar," she said, with something akin to a smile. "But it's coming back. Little by little."

He walked over, grabbed a small chair, and pulled it close to her. As he sat, he jokingly said, "So, what have you been up to. Raising hell, I bet."

That elicited a bit of a grin, followed by an explanation of the mechanical paraphernalia she found herself in. He listened intently. Asking questions about one function or another. When it seemed that her side of the conversation was lagging, he began to tell her of some of the individuals he had known in the military who had endured critically life-changing injuries. How the revitalization of their spirit had been every bit as important as their physical recuperation. He doubted, at least so soon after her injury, that she shared his optimism, but he wanted her to know he believed she could achieve contentment and happiness regardless of her physical condition.

Talk of the future however, eventually turned to the past. She told him she could remember him, but not necessarily how they had met, why, or what they had or hadn't done. He concocted a story about being a dressage fan, and that their appreciation of horses had brought them together. She surprised him completely when, without warning, she asked "Were we ever lovers?"

Pausing for a moment, he said, "Once… in a place by the sea."

Her demeanor gave no clue as to whether she remembered or not. If she did, she chose to keep her thoughts to herself. If she didn't, Ellis concluded, nothing would be gained by pursuing it.

Their interlude ended, much as it had at the Del, with Alex simply saying, "I'm tired now. I'd like to rest."

Ellis was about to ask if he could get her anything or help in any way, but the press of the button, the whirring sound and the chair turning away from him, signaled an end to their brief encounter. Before he turned and started for the door, he did say, "I hope we can get together again one of these days… if you'd like that." No reply was forthcoming. He simply added, "Goodbye." It too was met with silence.

~ ~ ~ ~ ~

McCullum was writing at the desk in his study when the housekeeper announced that Mr. Ellis was there to see him. Without looking up, he said, "Emelda, show Mr. Ellis in and then give that tradesman waiting out front the go ahead to do what I asked."

"Yes, Mr. McCullum," she dutifully replied.

The room had been restored to its former grandeur. Books back in their shelves. Furniture repaired or replaced. Globe, returned to its refurbished axis. Window, stunning as it was before. The only thing that seemed different to Ellis, was the absence of the stand in the shape of a crown and the glass case that sat atop it with twelve miniature palominos inside. Nothing had been brought in to replace it. Things had simply been shifted enough to cover the fact that anything had ever been there.

Head down, pen in hand, he said, "Have a seat Mr. Ellis. Just be a second." A few moments later, he set his writing instrument aside, looked up at his guest and remarked, "Have to write everything down these days. Make sure I don't forget. Damned nuisance, but a necessity. Don't ever get old, lad. There's no future in it."

"Place looks great," Ellis said. "Like nothing ever happened."

"Yes. I wanted it all put back together as soon as possible. Amazing what a little encouragement and a lot of money will do to supercharge repairs. So, did you see Alex?"

"I did."

"She recognize you?"

"Yes and no."

"Don't take it personally. What with the accident and the medication and all, well, she even has trouble knowing me every now and then."

Ellis asked, "Is there any chance of her getting better?"

"With luck and hard work, she might get off the ventilator and be able to breathe on her on one day. No way she'll ever be getting out of that chair, however. And the schizophrenia just gets medicated, not cured."

An abrupt silence indicated neither man wanted to pursue that conversation any further. McCullum broke from the lull before Ellis.

"So. Glad you consented to come over. Had something I wanted to talk to you about."

"Actually, *I* called and made the appointment to see you and Alex."

"You did? Well, I guess coincidences actually do happen. What did you want to see me about?"

"Ah… why don't you go first," Ellis answered. "Why did you want to see me?"

Going first was no problem for McCullum. He'd been doing so for most of his life.

"Mr. Ellis, I want you to come to work for me. Full time. Right here. Want to give you the job Skeffington had. Ramrod. Straw boss. Head of security. Overseer of everything I don't have the time or the patience to oversee. You'll have a place to live—rent free—all the food the cook can cook, any time you're hungry—at no cost—and days off whenever you want to take them. Plus a salary that will make your head swim."

"I'm not—"

"You really owe it to me, you know. I mean you did away with my number one man."

"He was trying to do away with me."

"Well, the best man won, didn't he? That's why I want you on my payroll. What do you say?"

"I'm going to decline your offer."

"Paid vacation every year… to anywhere you want to go. I'd pick up the cost."

"I like being my own boss."

"Bonuses… not only Christmas… but all the damn holidays."

"I appreciate your faith in me… and your generous offer… but I'm going to have to say no."

"Want to know what the salary is?"

"No."

"I have it written down on this paper. Let's say we double it."

"Let's say we don't."

"My word, Ellis! Isn't there anything I can do to bring you onboard?"

"There is not."

"Well I'll be damned. Do you have any idea how many people would jump at an opportunity like the one I'm offering you?"

"I'm sure I can't count that high."

An involuntary chuckle preceded McCullum saying, "Ellis, you are a pip. A certified pip."

"Never been called *that* before. I'll take it as a compliment."

"It was meant to be. All right, sir. I know when I'm not wanted. So let's move on. What the hell did you want to see me about?"

"I wanted to return this."

Ellis reached inside his coat pocket and pulled out two banded stacks of hundred dollar bills. He put them on the desk in front of McCullum. Then he reached inside his other pocket, pulled out two more stacks and put them down beside the first two.

"And just what is this," the elder man asked.

"It's $36,000 of the $50,000 dollars you paid me to secure the palomino. The rest went to a more than reasonable fee for me, operating expenses incurred while working with… shall we say… less than scrupulous individuals in Mexico, plus medical expenses relating to this beauty mark on the side of my head."

"You are saying you don't want the money?"

"I'm saying I shouldn't have accepted that much in the first place. I was blinded by your largess. I should have been the one to set the fee. I've been adequately compensated. Consider this return of an overpayment."

"Amazing. You sure you're not going to hate yourself in the morning?"

"Probably. But I'll feel swell about myself tonight."

"Is that it, then? Is that all you wanted with me," McCullum asked.

"That's all. I'll be going now."

"You can't leave."

"I can't. Why not?"

"That dismal rental you showed up in isn't here anymore."

"Sure it is. I've got the keys in my pocket."

"Mail them back. I had the car picked up. It's being taken to the rental company."

Ellis wasn't sure what to say, do, or think. He opted for, "And just how am I supposed to get back to San Diego?"

"Your vehicle's in the driveway. Here are the keys," McCullum said, as he reached in the top drawer of his desk, pulled them out, and tossed them to Ellis who had no choice but to catch them in midair.

"I was informed about what happened to your car. If you can set your own fees Mr. Ellis, surely I can give a bonus for a job well done."

Ellis looked closely at the fob on the sterling silver key ring. The engraving read *To B E from C T M. Horse power to remember me by.* He looked up at McCullum, who spoke before the P. I. could get a word out.

"When you reach my age, Mr. Ellis, you'll understand that it's quite comforting to have certain people think well of you... during whatever time you have left above ground... and perhaps even more so when you're below it. In days to come, It will give me great pleasure to know that you're likely thinking kindly of me each time you get behind the wheel."

Ellis tried to interject with "Sir, I really can't—"

McCullum cut him off again. "Please son, do an old fogy a favor. Help me think I can still put a smile on a good man's face."

Ellis wasn't sure what to say, but he was without a car, and a private eye without a car in California is about as useful as a jockey without a mount in the Kentucky Derby. So he simply said, "Thanks."

The housekeeper escorted him to the front door, opened it, and Ellis stepped outside. There, in the driveway, was a gleaming white 1966 230 SL Mercedes coupe. It didn't just look like the one he used to be in love with, it looked better.

A few minutes later, driving down the winding path that would take him back to the main highway, Ellis determined that he had not really compromised his principals by accepting the classic car. Of course, the smooth handling, effortless acceleration, and his own rakish shadow fluttering in the wind, aided that assessment.

Top down, breeze tingling the scar on the side of his head, Ellis ran his hand along the upholstered leather seat. He looked at the slim, clean lines of the dash. He considered the fact that the car was almost sixty years old, and while it ran like new, and would take him to the city and wherever he needed to go, what it really did was help him fulfill a dream. A dream of preserving and perpetuating craftsmanship and elegance and achievement.

Maybe that's what McCullum was really doing, the P. I. began to ponder. Not just securing a prized gift for a grandson, or an incredibly valuable investment, or even art for its place in history. Maybe the pursuit of the twelve palominos was simply a way for one man to complete a personal quest, to fulfill a lifelong dream. Such are the thoughts that sunny California afternoons engender. But by the time Ellis reached the end of the private road, rain clouds had blown in from the sea causing him to reappraise his former reverie. Perhaps the best dreams, Ellis concluded, are those forever unfulfilled. Yet to achieve the desired outcome, they never result in pain, or tragedy, or sorrow. Unfulfilled dreams always end the same way. With hope.

ABOUT THE AUTHOR

JOE KILGORE HAS WON AWARDS for novels, novellas, screenplays, and short stories. His tales have appeared in magazines, creative journals, anthologies, and online literary publications. He is the author of *Misfortune's Wake* and *Insomniac: Short Stories for Long Nights*, as well as the Brig Ellis novels, *Fool's Errand, Dying Art, Cast Them Dead, Carrion Moon*, and *Twelve Palominos*. His other novels include *The Horse Killer, A Farmhouse in the Rain, The Blunder,* and *The Golden Dancer.*

Prior to writing fiction, Joe had a long and successful career creating, writing, and producing television and radio commercials, plus newspaper, magazine, and internet content for an international advertising agency. He also writes novel reviews professionally for national and international firms. He lives in Austin, Texas, with his wife, Claudia, an accomplished artist. You can read more about him and his writing at JoeKilgore.com.

www.ingramcontent.com/pod-product-compliance
Lightning Source LLC
LaVergne TN
LVHW091543060526
838200LV00036B/684